PURRFECT DOUBLE

THE MYSTERIES OF MAX 46

NIC SAINT

PURRFECT DOUBLE

The Mysteries of Max 46

Copyright © 2021 by Nic Saint

All rights reserved. No part of this book may be reproduced in any form by any electronic or mechanical means including photocopying, recording, or information storage and retrieval without permission in writing from the author.

This is a work of fiction. Names, characters, places, brands, media, and incidents are either the product of the author's imagination or are used fictitiously. The author acknowledges the trademarked status and trademark owners of various products referenced in this work of fiction, which have been used without permission. The publication/use of these trademarks is not authorized, associated with, or sponsored by the trademark owners.

Edited by Chereese Graves

www.nicsaint.com

Give feedback on the book at: info@nicsaint.com

facebook.com/nicsaintauthor
@nicsaintauthor

First Edition

Printed in the U.S.A

PURRFECT DOUBLE

Friend or Fowl

I'm not an investor, since cats don't hold stock or manage their own portfolios, but my understanding of a CEO is that they lead the company to ever higher pinnacles of success, which then reflects on the stock price. So when Cotton Karat, CEO of the luxury goods Karat Group started canoodling with his supermodel girlfriend on stage during the group's annual shareholders' meeting, it's safe to say his frivolous behavior didn't go down well with investors. Soon the man was found murdered in a rather gruesome way. Only it quickly transpired that not all was what it seemed.

And then of course there was my friend Dooley, looking for a way to ingratiate himself with Odelia before the baby arrived. As he saw it, I'm the brains of Odelia's cat contingent, Harriet the beauty, and Brutus the brawn. So what is his USP? As it turns out, not a very appealing one. On top of that, Gran had recently converted to vegetarianism, and decided that the rest of the family should follow in her footsteps. Suffice it to say things quickly turned unpalatable.

CHAPTER 1

The Karat Group's annual shareholders' meeting didn't exactly go as planned. The shareholders were all there, and so was the chairman of the board, Diedrich Karat, but the star of the show was of course current CEO Cotton Karat. Or at least he should have been, as he was expected to lead the meeting and discuss both the group's past year's financial results as well as future expected earnings and projections. Instead, all he seemed interested in was to salivating over his new girlfriend, the delectable Ebony Pilay.

Many a shareholder, from the lowliest ones, with only a few Karat Group shares in their investment portfolio, to the biggest specimens, proud to own a large chunk of the company, was stunned as the meeting progressed, and the group's current leader couldn't keep his eyes or his hands off his supermodel girlfriend. The fact alone that he'd placed her center stage for this all-important event was a blatant departure from tradition.

As far as the collected shareholders, and the denizens of the financial press were aware, Ebony Pilay, though a well-known fashion model, owned no Karat Group shares, nor did she play any part in the group's organizational structure. She wasn't a CEO, CFO, COO or any of the other acronyms one often sees bandied about in the *Wall Street Journal*. Her only claim to that most coveted position next to the CEO was that she was his girlfriend. And Cotton Karat, the third scion of the Karat family to lead the luxury goods group, made sure no one could forget it. Lovey-dovey was one way to describe the scene.

It led to several members of the press corps to titter without inhibition, which was a strange spectacle to be sure. Usually the dreariest of journos, absolutely devoid of a sense of humor, and only perking up when being asked to write about interest rates or the price-to-earnings ratio, they now behaved as if they were all writing for the *National Enquirer*, ears red and eyes glittering with glee at this awful train wreck in progress.

Diedrich Karat, Cotton's dad and the group's previous CEO, looked as if he was barely hanging on to his equanimity. He'd already engaged in a bout of furious whisperings with the group's legal advisor Tobias Pushman, but what could they do? They couldn't berate Cotton in public, or frogmarch his girlfriend off the stage. The rest of the group's main players, all gathered on that stage, seemed to have accepted their role in the drama, and adopted a policy of grinning and bearing it and trying to act as if this was the most natural thing in the world, and not a complete meltdown of one of the country's biggest concerns.

The Karat Group's stock was trading at a thousand dollars a share at the start of the meeting. By the time the meeting finally adjourned, the stock had dropped to five hundred a share. One hundred billion dollars in value had been erased from the market cap. In other words: the single-largest drop in share price since the crash of 2001.

"Have you completely lost your mind?!"

"It's just a dip, Dad," Cotton said.

"A dip? A DIP?!"

Tobias Pushman, the group's legal beagle, gave his former boss and current chairman of the board a look of concern. Diedrich's face had turned the color of a ripe tomato. Drops of sweat were beading the man's brow and skipping down his temples, and his hair was matted to his sizable dome. If his blood pressure kept rising, a coronary was a given.

"Sir, I think you better sit down," Tobias suggested.

"I won't sit down until this matter is resolved and resolved to my satisfaction!" Diedrich thundered, swinging his arms dangerously. "Do you realize what you've done? You've singlehandedly wrecked the group! Reduced us to a Wall Street laughingstock!"

"You're exaggerating, Dad," said Cotton, who'd placed his sneakered feet up on his desk and was throwing a stress ball into the air with his left hand and deftly catching it with his right. "So the stock dropped a couple of points. It'll self-correct. You'll see."

"It won't self-correct," said Diedrich, shaking with righteous anger at so much ignorance. "It will self-destruct if you keep fornicating with this… this… this Jezebel!"

"Hey, Ebony is a highly respected and extremely successful model, Dad. Twenty *Vogue* covers and counting. And we weren't fornicating. We were merely displaying our mutual affection."

"It's not done, son! You can't organize a petting session at the annual shareholders' meeting!"

"It's not a good look," Tobias agreed.

Diedrich threw a copy of the *Wall Street Journal* onto his

son's desk. The headline screamed, 'Cotton Kills Karat.' "If you keep this up, we're toast, Cotton. Toast!"

"I'm sure it's not as bad as all that," Cotton tut-tutted.

"It's worse! They're predicting we'll be ripe for a hostile takeover bid before the end of the next fiscal quarter. Our shareholders are all threatening to sue!"

Cotton rolled his eyes. He didn't seem overly concerned. On his desk, a framed picture of Ebony Pilay held pride of place. It was the first of many *Vogue* covers she'd graced with her willowy presence, and she was staring into the lens as lusciously as she had gazed at Cotton at that fateful meeting.

"Just imagine if Warren Buffett brought a supermodel to Berkshire Hathaway's annual meeting," said Diedrich, "and instead of talking about the value of the company portfolio spent two hours canoodling with his girlfriend instead! The man would be vilified!"

"Now you're simply being dramatic," said Cotton as he aimed the ball at a mini basketball hoop in the corner of his office and hit it on the first try. "And now if you'll both excuse me, I've got a lunch date with Ebony, and the lady doesn't like to be kept waiting."

And watched on by his dumbfounded dad and his apoplectic legal advisor, the youngest CEO in the business left the room, carelessly humming *'You're still the one.'*

For a moment, silence reigned in the room, then Diedrich turned a look of desperation to the man whose legal acumen was only rivaled by his unparalleled knack for designing daring schemes, and said, "Give me something, Tobias. Anything."

Tobias, a swarthy man with thick brows that concealed

two cold blue eyes, steepled his fingers and brought them to his lips. "I think I might have an idea for you, sir."

"What is it?"

"It's a little risky, but it might offer a solution for all of our problems."

"Does it involve murdering Cotton and making it look like an accident?"

"Not exactly, sir. Though it does involve putting him on ice for a little while."

Diedrich allowed himself to drop down in one of the wingback chairs in the big office. His face was still an unhealthy shade of puce, and judging from the veins throbbing in his neck, the man was in urgent need of his blood pressure medication. "What did you have in mind?"

"Have you ever seen a French comedy named 'Le Con,' sir?"

"I'm not really into French comedy, though I have a feeling I'm in one right now. Though it could also be a French horror movie."

"In the movie, the CEO of one of those big French conglomerates finds himself at the center of some serious fracas, so his assistant comes up with the brilliant idea of replacing him with a double. The double is just a nobody, of course, with no real powers or authority. A puppet, if you will, controlled by the company's board of directors."

"A double?"

The sharpest legal mind ever to graduate from NYU nodded earnestly. "We ship Cotton off to the Heartfield Clinic, where he can be cured of his sex addiction. We buy off Miss Pilay so she will sever all ties with Cotton, and while your son is safely tucked away at Heartfield, a double takes his place, his every decision controlled by us."

"I see," said Diedrich thoughtfully. "And where do you propose we find this idiot?"

The lawyer's lips formed a devious moue. "Oh, I have one lined up for us already, sir."

CHAPTER 2

Eric Blandine was a man as bland as his name suggested. He was a lowly worker drone who'd spent his entire adult life stocking tins of foie gras, drums of caviar and boxes of exclusive pralines in one of the many warehouses that furnished these delicacies to airport stores and gift shops supplied by the Karat Group. And he was just fulfilling a large order of foie gras and boxing them up for imminent shipment when a low whistle sounded in his rear. He turned, and found himself looking at his buddy James Perkins.

"Boss wants to see you, Goldie," said Jimmy with a cheeky grin.

Due to Eric's uncanny resemblance to Cotton Karat, his colleagues had gotten into the habit of referring to him with the unoriginal nickname Goldie, short for karat gold.

"What does he want to see me for?" asked Eric, who didn't like to be disturbed when he was boxing up an order. He was one of those people who liked to do things the proper way, and being interrupted like this irked his sense of appropriate order and protocol.

"Your girlfriend probably dropped by," said Jimmy.

"Girlfriend?" asked Eric, carefully descending the metal ladder and balancing the half-filled box in the crook of his elbow.

"Ebony, of course. Though to be honest I don't know what she sees in you, Goldie."

"Must be all of his billions," said Margie, another one of Eric's colleagues. She stood leaning against the rack, taking a break.

"Or his sex appeal," said Jimmy. "Let's not forget about Goldie's amazing sex appeal."

"Did you see him at that meeting the other day?" asked Margie.

"What meeting?" asked Eric, good-naturedly going along with the gentle ribbing. He was used to it by now, and didn't mind.

"That big shareholders' meeting. Goldie here kissing and fondling Ebony in front of a room full of stiffs. Looked like he was having a great old time, weren't you, Goldie?"

"Oh, absolutely," said Eric as he carefully placed down the box. "A wonderful time."

"I wonder what Maisie thinks about all this, though," said Jimmy, referring to Eric's wife.

"I'll bet she's fine with it," said Margie. "She's a forgiving wife, our Maisie is."

"She certainly is," said Eric with a smile.

"What do you think you're doing!" suddenly a voice rang out through the warehouse. "Get a move on, Blandine! The boss don't got all day, you know!"

"Yeah, hop to it, Goldie," Margie urged him on. "Let's not keep Ebony waiting."

"I'm coming!" Eric cried, and hurried off, watched on by his grinning colleagues.

He entered the office, fully expecting to find Norm there,

eager to discuss the plans for his upcoming vacation, but instead he found Norm accompanied by two men he'd never seen before, though one of them looked slightly familiar for some reason.

"Eric, please take a seat," said Norm, and gestured to a chair in front of his desk.

"Yes, sir," said Eric meekly, and quickly sat down, nervously rubbing his hands on his blue jumpsuit as he did.

Much to his surprise, he found the older of the two visitors eyeing him closely. The man, who was probably in his early sixties, and had one of those big flabby faces, even brought his face so close to his that he could smell the cigar smoke emanating from him.

"Mh," said the man finally. "You were right, Tobias. It is uncanny."

"Isn't it?" said the other man. He was dressed in an expensive suit, was clean-shaven and had one of those square jaws that reminded Eric of a G-man. He also had heavy brows that half-obscured two sharp eyes that were coldly scrutinizing him. Like a fishmonger studying a halibut and deciding how best to slice and dice it for later consumption.

"Eric," said Norm, "these two gentlemen have a special request for you."

"Oh?" said Eric, wondering if they were here to place a large order of foie gras.

"Do you know who I am?" asked the older man.

"No, sir," said Eric truthfully.

"This is Diedrich Karat," said Norm.

Eric stared at the man. Then his eyes traveled to the large picture suspended on the wall behind Norm. It was the same man, only looking slightly younger and a lot skinnier. Eric's eyes went wide. "Mr. Karat?" he asked, his voice sounding squeaky to his own ears.

"That's right," said Mr. Karat, nodding with satisfaction at the other man's consternation.

"Has anyone ever told you that you are the spitting image of Mr. Karat's son Cotton, Eric?" asked the younger man, who hadn't yet been introduced.

Eric nodded wordlessly.

"His colleagues all call him Goldie," said Norm. "For karat gold?" he added when the two men turned bland faces to him.

"Is that so?" said Mr. Karat with a sort of avuncular smile that didn't quite become him. Like a shark trying to affect a grin at its prey. "Well, I don't know if you're aware of this, Eric, but my son has recently found himself in a spot of trouble."

Once again Eric nodded wordlessly. He now realized he was clenching his buttocks to a painful extent, and that his armpits were twin pools of sweat. It's not every day that you suddenly find yourself in the presence of the big boss of your company.

"Cotton needs to go away for a couple of weeks, Eric," the G-man took over the narrative. "And in the meantime we would like you to replace him."

Eric's butt-clenching intensified. "You would?" he squeaked.

"Only for a couple of weeks, mind you," said Mr. Karat. "While Cotton works through a few issues that are of no concern to you."

"But..." Eric began, but was immediately silenced by a look of warning from Norm.

"You'd be doing the company a huge favor," said the G-man.

"It's important that no one find out about Cotton disappearing from the scene," Mr. Karat explained. "Our investors might get antsy. They're like vultures, you see. One sign of weakness and they're likely to attack and rip the flesh from our bones."

"And that's where you come in," said the G-man, towering over Eric, as was Mr. Karat. If they'd have aimed a spotlight at his face he wouldn't have been surprised. "We need you to make sure things at the Karat Group look as if it's all business as usual. Though of course we'll shield you off as much as we can. All you need to do is look the part."

"B-b-but..." sputtered Eric.

"*Look* the part but not *act* the part. I mean in meetings or negotiations with clients."

"We'll take care of all that," Mr. Karat assured him. "All you have to do is show up and make it look as if Cotton is right where he should be, in complete control of the company."

"We don't have to tell you that discretion is an absolute necessity," said the other man.

"You're not to breathe a word about this to anyone, you hear?" said Mr. Karat.

"Not to your wife, not to your friends or colleagues. Absolutely no one."

"And when all is said and done, you'll be handsomely rewarded."

Eric's ears pricked up. "Rewarded?" he squeaked.

"Handsomely."

He swallowed as he thought about this for a moment. "I'm not sure if..." he began.

"Eric, this is not a proposition," said Norm warningly. "This is an assignment."

"The most important assignment you'll ever get," said Mr. Karat.

"I don't know about this..." he muttered helplessly.

The two men converged on him, their combined bulk making him shrink and cower. "You want to help your employer, don't you, Eric?" said Mr. Karat. "Be a loyal company man?"

"Well, of course, but…"

"Stock options," said the G-man with a cold smile as his eyes bored into Eric's.

"Yes, we'll give you stock options," said Mr. Karat. "Stock options that will make you a very rich man indeed, Mr. Blandine. Stock options that will ensure a future for you and for your family. An unencumbered future for you and your loved ones. How does that sound?"

"Good," he admitted as he wondered if he'd ever be able to go to the bathroom again.

"This is not a negotiation, Blandine," said Norm, as he also got up from behind his desk and joined the browbeating exercise. "This is an order. You will pretend to be Cotton Karat from now on, and you will not mention this to anyone. Is that clear?!"

He meekly nodded. It was perfectly clear. The only problem was: how was he ever going to explain all this to Maisie?

※

"I don't get it," said Maisie as she used a cotton pad to remove the makeup from her face. "Why do you have to go on a training weekend?"

"Not a weekend," Eric patiently explained, seated on the bed. "It's a training month."

"I've never heard such nonsense in my entire life. Why does a warehouse worker have to go train for a month? What are they going to teach you? How to print labels?"

"It's because of my promotion, Maisie," said Eric. "I already explained this to you."

"And I'm telling you I don't believe a word you're telling me. So try again, and this time please don't insult me and tell me the truth for a change."

"It is the truth, sweetheart. Norm called me into his office today and said I'm being promoted. From now on I'm going to be team leader. And all team leaders have to train for a month in Garden City. It's standard company policy."

Maisie made a skeptical noise as she studied her face in the mirror. She was a large woman, with coarse features and a square doughy face. But even though she wasn't exactly pretty, she was the apple of Eric's eye, and had been since the day they met in high school. It wasn't so much that they'd fallen in love at first sight and had become high school sweethearts, but more that one day Maisie decided Eric would make a suitable husband and father to her kids and told him that from now on she was his girlfriend. And Eric, meek as usual, had simply accepted her dictum. Not that he had a lot of choice in the matter. When Maisie made a decision, that was the way it was, no back talk allowed.

She now fixed her husband with a curious look. "You're lying to me, Eric."

"No, I'm not," he said weakly.

"I can tell from the way your nose is twitching. It's your tell."

"My nose isn't twitching," he said quietly, as his hand surreptitiously traveled to the traitorous appendage and took a firm hold of his schnoz.

Maisie planted both hands on her hips, a clear sign she was fed up with this nonsense. "Enough of this, Blandine. You better start telling me the truth in one—two—three…"

"All right, all right!" he finally cried. "Mr. Karat and his lawyer were in the office today, and they told me I have to pretend to be Cotton Karat for a couple of weeks, while Cotton is off to some clinic somewhere to get cured of his sex addiction. They don't want anyone to find out about it since it might sink the stock price even further than it's already sunk and because I look so much like Cotton they chose me to be his double."

Whatever Maisie had expected, it clearly wasn't this. But the story was so unlikely, so outrageous, so crazy, that it simply had to be true. "Well, I'll be damned," she finally said.

"They're giving me stock options," Eric said, not meeting his wife's gaze. "A lot of stock options. And if I manage to pull this off, and make the stock go up again, I'll be a rich man. Or so they said."

"How much?" said Maisie curtly. She wasn't the kind of woman to hem and haw, but as usual went straight to the heart of the matter.

"Ten stock options at five hundred dollars a share. If the stock starts trading at last week's price again, they'll be worth ten thousand."

"And if they keep sinking, they'll be worth zilch." She thought for a moment. "What about Ebony Pilay?"

"She's out of the picture. They bought her off."

Maisie uttered an incredulous laugh. "Of course they did. And I'll bet they offered her a lot more than ten measly stock options."

Eric shrugged. "It wasn't a negotiation, sweetheart. It was either this or I wasn't going to have a job anymore. Plus they'd blackball me. Make sure I won't find a job elsewhere."

She thought for a moment, then finally nodded, her black eyes glittering. "You'll go through with this, and when you're halfway through the assignment you'll ask for another ten options." And when her husband started to protest she held up her hand. "Don't you see? They need you more than you need them. How many Cotton lookalikes do you think there are in this country? They must be desperate to hatch such a ridiculous scheme." She rubbed her hands. "This is our chance to make some serious moolah. Lots and lots of it."

Eric sighed and let himself drop down on the bed.

He had a feeling his troubles had only just begun.

CHAPTER 3

I was peacefully sleeping at the foot of Odelia's bed and dreaming of some prime kibble when suddenly a loud scream brutally tore through the gossamer cobweb of my dream. The scream seemed to come from somewhere close by, and when I opened my eyes and lifted my head, I saw that it was actually Odelia herself who was screaming!

Immediately I rose up and padded across the bed to find out what was going on. Was the baby she was carrying kicking up a fuss? Had Odelia had a nightmare and had it thrown her for a loop? When you live with a human you soon realize anything is possible.

But when I joined her, I saw that she was staring at something on her pillow in horror. It wasn't Chase, for he was now supporting himself on one elbow and staring at the same spot, his face also contorted in abject shock.

And then I saw it: a mouse, placed neatly on the edge of Odelia's pillow.

Dooley, who'd been resting alongside me, now also came trotting up. He was smiling, and when I glanced over to him, he gave me a wink!

"It's a mouse," said Chase dully. As a detective, that was some quick thinking on his part.

"I can see it's a mouse," said Odelia. "But what is it doing there?"

"It looks dead," said Chase, as he gave the critter a gentle nudge with his finger.

"I don't get it," said Odelia. "So it crawled up onto my pillow in the middle of the night and then died?"

Both she and Chase now looked in my direction, as if expecting an explanation from yours truly. I could see why, of course. I'm a cat, you see, and cats are well known for being in the habit of catching mice and depositing them wherever takes their fancy.

"I didn't put it there," I assured them. "In fact I've never seen this mouse before."

To be absolutely honest, I'm not one for all this mouse-catching business. I always say live and let live, and that goes for every living creature under the sun—even mice.

"I put that mouse on your pillow," suddenly Dooley piped up, and he even looked proud as he spoke these immortal words.

"Dooley!" Odelia cried. "What the hell!"

Dooley's smile faltered. "I thought you'd like it," he said in his defense.

"You thought I'd enjoy finding a dead mouse on my pillow?!"

"Well…" he said. "Most humans seem to like it."

"Oh, Dooley," Odelia sighed as she stared at the offending dead animal some more.

"Did Dooley put it there?" asked Chase.

"He did. He thought it was a good idea."

"Have you been watching the Discovery Channel again?" I asked my friend.

Dooley nodded, looking a little shamefaced now. "There

was a documentary on last night. About how cats always bring their humans little presents. Like mice and birds and... and worms and such. And the humans in the documentary seemed to like it."

"I'll bet they did," I said, shaking my head.

Odelia regretted her harsh rebuke when she saw Dooley's discomfiture. So she patted my friend's head and said, "It's very sweet of you to bring me a present, Dooley, but you didn't have to do that." She eyed him more closely. "Tell me you didn't kill that mouse?"

"Of course not!" said Dooley, horrified at the idea. "It was dead when I found it."

"Good," said Odelia. Clearly she didn't like the idea of her sweet cats turning into a couple of nocturnal predators all of a sudden.

"Where did you find it?" I asked, curious.

"In the field behind the house," said Dooley.

"It died a natural death," Odelia assured her husband.

Chase grunted something under his breath. He didn't seem overly concerned whether the mouse had died from old age or from an attack by some ravenous stalker. "I'll get rid of it," he said, and picked the mouse up by its tail, then carried it off, presumably to dump it in the compost bin for later disposal and subsequent recycling.

"Don't you think we should return it where Dooley found it?" I asked. "That mouse has a mother and a father, and sisters and brothers, who are probably wondering where it went off to all of a sudden."

"Better put it in the field," Odelia instructed her husband. "Let nature take its course."

"It will attract other, bigger animals," Chase warned.

Odelia shrugged. "We could give it a proper burial," she suggested.

Chase grinned, still holding the mouse between thumb and index finger. "A proper burial for a mouse?"

"It's a living, breathing creature, Chase. It deserves our respect."

Chase inspected the dead mouse. I had the impression he wanted to point out it wasn't breathing or living anymore, but he wisely refrained from stating the obvious. Instead, he said, "I'll stick it in the fridge for now. We can bury it later on."

And since Odelia and Chase were up, they decided to get ready for their day. The sun had hoisted itself over the horizon and was casting its rays into the room. Rise and shine!

"I don't get it," I told Dooley while Odelia took a shower and Chase rummaged around in search of a suitable coffin for the mouse. "Why would you think it's a good idea to put a dead mouse on Odelia's pillow?"

"It's the baby," my friend explained, looking pained. "Once the baby is born, it's going to take up a big chunk of Odelia's time and attention. And then what about me?"

"She'll still have time for us," I said. "It's not as if she'll suddenly forget all about us."

"She won't forget about you," Dooley clarified. "Because you're her favorite."

"I'm not her favorite," I said with a laugh.

"Oh, yes, you are. You solve crimes and make her look good. You're her ace sleuth, Max."

"Okay, so what about Harriet and Brutus? They're not ace sleuths and Odelia loves them just as much as she loves us."

"She loves Harriet because she's pretty, and Brutus because he's big and strong. But me? I don't have any special qualities, Max. I'm not smart like you, I'm not pretty like Harriet, and I'm not big and strong like Brutus. I'm... superfluous."

I was taken aback, both from hearing Dooley use such a difficult word, and by the meaning behind it. "You're not superfluous, Dooley. You're... sweet and cuddly."

He gave me a skeptical look. "Please. Sweet and cuddly is not an admirable quality."

"It is! And you're very sweet and very cuddly, Dooley."

But he didn't seem convinced. "I need a USP, Max."

"You mean UPS, surely?"

"No, I need a unique selling proposition. You and Harriet and Brutus all have one, and I also need one, or the moment that baby is born, they'll simply chuck me out."

"Nobody is going to chuck you out, Dooley."

"They will, unless I make myself indispensable. Which is why I thought of that mouse."

"I very much doubt you'll make yourself indispensable by festooning Odelia's pillow with dead mice."

"Yeah, she didn't seem to like it all that much, did she?"

"No, she did not."

We both looked on as Odelia removed the cover from the pillow and dumped it into the laundry basket, then picked up the pillow, thought for a moment, and dumped that into the laundry basket, too. Then she removed the cover from the duvet and put that in the laundry, and finally ended up putting both her and Chase's duvets into the laundry, as well as the mattress cover, and if Chase hadn't entered the room and stopped her, I had the impression she would have stripped the mattress off the bed, too, for deep cleaning.

No, Dooley's new USP wasn't exactly a big hit with this expectant mother.

CHAPTER 4

Dooley and I were tucking into our first kibble of the day when a special news bulletin caught Odelia and Chase's attention. As usual, the TV had been blaring away in a corner of the kitchen, supplying some pleasant background noise while our humans prepared breakfast for themselves, when Chase turned up the sound.

"Well-known business tycoon Cotton Karat conducted his annual shareholders' meeting, but had more eyes for his girlfriend's bottom than for his company's bottom line," the newscaster intoned with visible glee. Footage of Cotton Karat kissing a stunning brunette supplied images to the newscaster's words. "Shareholders were less than impressed, and major shareholder Elvis Diamond even threatened legal action if Cotton doesn't stop acting like a lovesick puppy and more like the businessman he's supposed to be. Karat Group shares dropped like a stone, shaving off billions of dollars from the company's value." The newscaster now turned to his co-host. "What do you think, Karen? Would you buy from a man who is as loved up as Cotton Karat clearly is?"

"Absolutely not, Mike. If a man devotes all of his time to

his girlfriend and none of it to his company, why would he expect me to buy his products? He obviously doesn't care."

"Ouch. Looks like Cotton lost himself another customer."

The news bulletin turned to the weather forecast, and Chase turned down the sound.

"What do they sell, this Karat Group?" he asked as he buttered a piece of toast.

"Luxury stuff, mainly," said Odelia. "Caviar, foie gras, expensive cigars... But also jewelry and designer clothes, watches, purses... Anything that we can't afford," she finished with a rueful smile.

"Looks like they can afford to lose a couple of billion in revenue."

"Not sure they can. Ever since Cotton Karat took over from his dad, it's been one PR disaster after another. Frankly the investors and shareholders are getting fed up."

"Well, as long as they don't kill each other over it, I don't care," said the cop as he took a sip from his piping hot coffee.

"I actually interviewed Cotton Karat a couple of months ago," said Odelia, taking a seat at the kitchen counter. "He seemed like a nice enough guy. A real playboy, though. Seemed more interested in showing off his fancy car collection and his latest supermodel girlfriend than the company he's supposed to be running."

Just then, suddenly the glass sliding door opened and Odelia's dad walked in. He was looking a little wild-eyed and was anxiously glancing behind him as if he was a character in a Robert Ludlum novel, being persecuted by some nefarious government conspiracy.

Without a word, he made a beeline for Odelia's fridge, yanked it open and rummaged around until he found what he was looking for: a sizable sausage. He then cut a big chunk off the sausage, and still without a word of explanation, popped it into his mouth, closed his eyes in relish, and chewed on the delicacy as if it was a spoonful of Karat caviar.

"Dad!" said Odelia with a laugh. "What's going on?"

"Vegetarians," said Tex with a dark look in the direction of the door. Like Jason Bourne, his attackers could presumably enter through that door at any moment, eager to kill him.

"Vegetarians?" asked Odelia. "What are you talking about?"

"Your grandmother has gone over to the dark side," said the doctor, continuing to be mystifying. When the others merely stared at him, he said, "She's become a vegetarian."

"Poor Dad," said Chase with a chuckle. "You mean you're not allowed to eat meat anymore?"

Tex nodded, as he eyed the rest of that sausage eagerly.

"Eat it," Odelia suggested. "There's plenty more where that came from."

"Are you sure?" said Chase. "We don't want him to break the vegetarian's pledge."

Tex gave his son-in-law a dark look. "It's not as if I've got a choice. She's making me eat tofu," he said. "Can you imagine? Tofu!"

"I like tofu," said Odelia. "It's very tasty."

"But I want chicken!" Tex cried. "And steak. And ribs. And sausage!" And to show us he wasn't lying, he didn't bother with the knife, but simply bit off a huge chunk of sausage and chomped down like a man wrecked on some desert island who hasn't eaten for days.

Just then, another person arrived on the scene. It was Gran, and when she caught sight of Tex, taking another big bite out of that sausage, her face took on a grim look. "Tex Poole!" she cried, planting her hands on her bony hips. "What did I tell you about eating meat!"

"That it's bad for me?" asked Tex sheepishly.

"Very bad," said Gran. "Both for your health and for the environment. Spit it out!" She held a hand in front of her son-in-law's face and we watched as Tex reluctantly spat out the half-chewed sausage into her hand. She then disposed of it and gave Odelia a nasty look. "And you!" she said, pointing a finger at her granddaughter, "should know better than to aid and abet a known meat addict!"

Odelia and Chase shared a look of surprise, but before they could respond, Gran was already stomping back to the door, a sad-looking Tex in her wake. "I've got a nice breakfast for you, Tex," Gran was saying. "Fully plant-based and filled with all of the necessary nutrients and vitamins, and none of those awful toxins that you only find in meat products." And after lobbing a warning look in our direction, she walked out.

"Poor Dad," said Odelia once the coast was clear again.

"Yeah, and poor us," said Chase. "Cause knowing your grandmother, she won't stop until she's converted this entire town into vegetarianism."

"Maybe I should have put that mouse on Tex's pillow," Dooley suggested. "I have a feeling he's going to need it."

"Please don't put any mice on anyone's pillow, Dooley," I said. "Whatever the Discovery Channel says, it's not a good idea."

"But it's my USP, Max," he said. "In fact it's the only USP I've got!"

CHAPTER 5

Breakfast over, Dooley and I ventured outside. "I just hope Gran won't try and convince us to switch to a plant-based diet," I said as we passed through the cat flap. "It's all good and well for humans, but cats are carnivores. We need our bits of meat."

"I don't know, Max," said Dooley. "I don't think that's necessarily true. When I was holding that mouse in my mouth, I thought about eating it, and I actually felt nauseous."

"That's because we're basically spoiled, pampered cats, Dooley. For a cat like Clarice, a nice fat mouse is like a delicacy." Then again, our friend Clarice will even eat rats almost as big as she is. She truly is a rare specimen.

Stretched out on the lawn, we found Harriet and Brutus, taking in some of that early morning sun that is so pleasant. The rays were tickling their bellies, and they looked as well-fed as only two pampered, spoiled cats can look. They also looked thoroughly bored, as their next words indicated.

"We're bored, Max," said Harriet, a pretty white Persian. "Don't you have a case for us to solve or something?"

"Yeah, Maxie baby," said Brutus, a butch, black cat, "a nice juicy murder case is exactly what we need right now."

"I found a dead mouse this morning," Dooley announced. "I put it on Odelia's pillow but she wasn't happy."

"This mouse," said Harriet, perking up, "was it bludgeoned to death? Poisoned with some obscure poison? Its throat cut? Shot at close range? Or even garroted, maybe?"

"None of the above," I said. "It probably died of old age."

Harriet sank back down again. "Oh," she said, quickly losing interest.

"I don't get it," said Brutus. "Usually you're knee-deep in some murder investigation, Max. So what's going on, huh? Why isn't there some hot suspect you're pursuing?"

"Because it isn't every day that a murder is committed in this town, Brutus," I said. "And a good thing, too. Imagine that people got murdered left, right and center every moment of every day. Hampton Cove would be homicide central and would become uninhabitable."

"Tell me there's some case you're working on, Max," Harriet pleaded. "Anything!"

"Nope," I said, also resuming a restful position on the lawn. "Nothing at all." And actually I liked it that way. I know that people think I'm some kind of feline sleuth or something, and that I'm not happy until I can sink my teeth into a case, but in fact that couldn't be further from the truth. All I want is to lead a quiet and peaceful life. Eat some kibble, take a nap, spend some time with my friends, eat some kibble, take another nap...

In other words: the circle of life.

"Look, I know we've been giving you a hard time," Brutus piped up. "Trying to compete with you and all of that stuff. But I'm here to tell you that from now on we'll be good."

I frowned at the cat. "What are you talking about?"

"I'm offering you a truce, Max! Let's work together, eh?"

"I thought we were working together."

"I thought so, too, but it's clear to me that you're holding out on us." He gave me a keen look. "What are you working on right now? A shooting? A stabbing? A hanging? What?!"

"Nothing!" I said. "I'm not working on anything right now!"

"Oh, don't be like that, Max," said Harriet. "Just tell us!"

"Yeah, talk to us, buddy. I promise we'll collaborate."

"All I'm working on right now is a nap scheme."

"A nap scheme?"

"Yes. I've been feeling a little weak lately, and it's left me wondering if I'm getting enough sleep. So now I'm wondering where to squeeze in another couple of hours."

Harriet shared a look of concern with her mate. "He's holding out on us," was Brutus's conclusion.

"I'm not holding out on you!"

"Look, Max," said Brutus. "I get it. You're smart. You're clever. In fact you're probably some kind of genius. I don't know how you do it, cause you don't look like a genius. In fact you look more like a big orange blob."

"Blorange blob," I muttered.

"So you've got a brain like Einstein inside a blorange blob body. It happens. I can't explain it, but it's probably one of those things. Like Cherry Coke or deep-fried butter on a stick. In other words: an anomaly. But I'm here to tell you that from now on you can count on me and Harriet to do your legwork for you."

"What are you talking about?" I asked.

"Like *Jake and the Fatman*? I'll be Jake and you're the Fatman." He grinned. "Or in your case more like the Fatcat."

"I don't get it," I said, frowning.

He sighed. "All great detectives have a loony sidekick," he said, gesturing to Dooley, "but they also have a team of dicks who hunt down clues, spy on suspects and generally get busy with the rough stuff. And that's where Harriet and I come in: we'll be your dicks. So you better start talking, buddy, cause this offer is a time-limited one. We're going to help you nail the perp, but only if you put your cards on the table and do it right now."

He gave me a warning look that spoke volumes.

Unfortunately, as appealing as his offer was, I had no case to offer him, and when I told him as much, he made a disgusted gesture with his paw. "You got a lot to learn, Maxie baby," he said finally. "For one thing, detective work is a team sport, not a solo venture. So if you don't get wise soon, this?" he said, gesturing between us, "is over before it started."

And so he and Harriet took their leave, presumably to go look for some hot case to pursue, and left me and Dooley to think about their words.

"Am I a loony sidekick, Max?" asked Dooley finally.

"Of course not, buddy," I said.

"I'm not?" asked Dooley, alarmed. "Why not?"

I stared at him. "You want to be my loony sidekick?"

"Of course!"

"Okay, then I guess you are."

The smile he gave me was something to behold. "Thanks, Max. So maybe that's my USP?"

"Of course, Dooley," I said, hoping I could finally get some nap time in now.

CHAPTER 6

As it turned out, my nap time was cut short when Odelia decided she needed us on an assignment in town. It wasn't a murder case, or even any kind of case. In fact it was just the kind of thing Odelia is good at: covering an event that is of interest to the general public. Or in other words: the people who buy the *Hampton Cove Gazette* and in so doing pay her bills.

And so it was that we arrived at Town Hall, where a local captain of industry was being awarded some kind of medal in recognition of his contributions to the economy. And much to my surprise, it was in fact Cotton Karat who was the recipient of this award as doled out by Mayor Butterwick.

The award ceremony was a boring and long-winded affair, with plenty of speeches by the Mayor as well as several council members. Politicians may be chosen for their eloquence as well as their managerial qualities, but that obviously didn't apply to the can of council members they'd opened today, as the only purpose their particular oratorial set of skills served was a soporific one. I only woke up to watch Cotton Karat, who was a handsome man in his early forties, being offered his medal and accepting it gratefully.

The man was dressed in a snazzy suit, his hair was neatly coiffed and his face bronzed, but when it finally came time for him to launch into a speech of his own, a man with thick, heavy brows stepped in, and said that Mr. Karat's time was precious, and unfortunately he had a prior engagement that needed his urgent attention.

And so the playboy businessman was whisked off before he could entertain us with his words of wisdom and his business acumen.

Once outside, we watched as he descended the stairs en route to his limo, but as he reached that safe haven of luxury, suddenly a woman tore herself away from a pack of spectators and approached the business leader. She was holding a can of some substance in her arms, and before anyone could stop her, she was hoisting it in the direction of Mr. Karat, dousing him with some sticky red liquid that looked a lot like blood!

"Murderer!" the woman was screaming. "Animal slaughterer! Nazi butcher!"

And suddenly out from the crowd, more people sprang forward, hoisting banners scribbled with slogans that echoed the blood-throwing woman's incendiary cries. They were like a flash mob from hell.

'Meat is murder,' read one, and 'Ducks are people, too,' another, while a third announced that 'Foie gras is a crime against humanity.'

It all seemed very staged, somehow, as if it wasn't real. But then suddenly two familiar figures popped onto the scene, also hoisting a banner. They were Gran and her best friend Scarlett Canyon! And the banner they held aloft read, 'Cotton Karat is a mass murderer!'

"Isn't that Gran?" asked Dooley.

"Yeah, it is," I said, much surprised.

"What is she saying?"

"Something about ducks," I said, though it was hard to make out exactly what it was she was shouting, since a lot of people were shouting a lot of stuff, not least of whom were the two bodyguards Cotton had brought along with him, and who were now ushering their charge into the waiting limo. But before they could whisk the man away to safety, he held up his hand to wave at his attacker for some reason, and give her a kindly smile.

Not exactly a hard-boiled business shark, I thought as I watched the scene unfold. More like Santa Claus giving the children who've come out to greet him a friendly wave.

While the limo drove off, the two bodyguards shouting something into their wrist mics, and jogging alongside the limo, not unlike the Secret Service when the President comes to town, Gran and her cronies kept screaming abuse at the departing tycoon.

"It's going to be very difficult to clean that upholstery," Dooley remarked.

"Yeah, especially since I have the impression that it was paint, not blood."

"You think?"

"Oh, absolutely."

Plenty of the fake blood had ended up on the sidewalk, which now looked as if a minor massacre had taken place there. We approached and took a sniff and indeed determined that it was paint. "Odd," said Dooley. "Why would they pour paint on that poor man?"

"I think it's a symbolic thing," I said.

"Symbolic, how?"

"They seem to think eating meat is tantamount to murder, and to emphasize the fact, they can't think of anything better to do than to pour a few gallons of fake blood on the person they deem guilty of this murder."

"Murder!" my friend cried.

"It is a fact that the chickens, turkeys, cows and other animals killed to provide nourishment to a large cross section of the population, are killed without their written approval. So in a sense you might consider this a crime against the animal kingdom."

This gave my friend food for thought, for I didn't hear from him for the next ten minutes.

The protesters, now without a target to direct their protest at, were rolling up their banners and quietly conversing amongst themselves. Odelia, who had strolled up and was interviewing a few of them, wanting to get their view on the recent events, kept a keen eye on her grandmother and Scarlett, and I could sense that a rebuke trembled on the intrepid reporter's lips. It's one thing to strictly forbid your son-in-law to eat meat, but quite another to be arrested for causing damage to public property. And that an arrest was imminent became obvious when the constabulary suddenly arrived on the scene. Belatedly, one might say, but to compensate for their tardiness they had arrived en masse.

Moments later, the protesters had been taken into custody, Gran and Scarlett included, and carted off into several paddy wagons, dispatched especially for the occasion.

And thus ended Gran's first protest.

"I wish I was a fly on the wall," said Odelia, "listening in when Uncle Alec discovers his people have just arrested his mother and her friend."

For some reason the prospect seemed to provide her with great joy, for she was grinning with obvious delight. I guess Odelia isn't much of a vegetarian herself.

The one thing I found myself wondering as we made to leave, was what had happened to Cotton's girlfriend the supermodel. If I had understood correctly from the news report, those two were inseparable. And receiving a signature honor like a medal doled out by the town mayor would be just the event for this Ebony Pilay to grace with her presence.

So where was she? Or had Cotton already dumped her and replaced the model with a newer model? Judging from the man's track record the notion wasn't a far-fetched one.

CHAPTER 7

Ebony was staring at her phone, her mind a whirlwind and her chest ravaged by a storm of emotions.

'I think it's time for us to take a break,' the text said. 'I'm sure you understand. Cotton.'

She'd read it three times already, and by the time she reached the end once more, that whirlwind raging in her head suddenly became focused and hot like a laser beam.

Dumped! The bastard had dumped her! By text, no less!

Gritting perfect teeth, the supermodel's perfect face spelled the perfect storm. And as her nails furiously clicked on her phone's screen, typing out an appropriately fiery response, she suddenly halted and made one of those quick decisions she was so famous for with anyone from top designers, photographers to fashion show stage managers.

Five minutes later she was zooming along in her silver Mini Cooper, making a mockery of the town's speeding laws, and another ten minutes later she pulled up outside the main offices of the Karat Group on the outskirts of Hampton Cove.

She waltzed into the building, paid no attention to the

receptionist's annoying yapping, and immediately set foot for her boyfriend's office, her high-heeled Louboutins clacking on the marble floor. The receptionist's shouts in her rear were like background noise as she steeled herself for the upcoming confrontation with the bastard. Then she threw the doors wide and stormed into the man's office.

Cotton was in conference with that weaselly lawyer of his, but she didn't care.

"How dare you!" she screamed as she placed her phone on his desk. "How dare you break up with me by text!"

"E-E-Ebony!" the man cried as he got up from behind his desk.

"You could at least have the guts to dump me in person!" she said, and assumed one of her favored positions: three-quarter turn, hip thrust out, chin up, hand resting on opposite hip. It was the pose she ended every show with, and which had earned her the title 'Queen of the catwalk.' Invariably a thunderous applause followed this stance, but today all it earned her was a blank stare from her lover and irate glances from the lawyer.

"But E-E-Ebony..." Cotton bleated helplessly.

She frowned at the man. She'd expected some fireworks, not this pitiful display of snivelly weakness. "Well?" she demanded. "What do you have to say for yourself?"

"I-I-I..." the man stuttered. He seemed to have gone through some sort of transformation, she saw. One in which his balls had been removed and replaced with jelly.

"It's another woman, isn't it? Who? I have a right to know!"

"No, no, nothing like that!" Cotton assured her as he seemed to hide behind his desk.

She walked around the desk, and now stood in front of him, studying him up close and personal. Then she frowned. "You look different," she said. She placed an imperious hand on his head and tossed his hair like a salad. "Your hair... did you cut it? And your eyes, they look different, too." She narrowed her own eyes. "Are you wearing colored contacts?"

"Y-y-yes," he stammered. "Yes, that's it. Colored contacts."

"Look, Miss Pilay," said the lawyer. "Cotton is a very busy man, so…"

"Something is not right," Ebony said finally. "What is it? It can't be another woman. There's no one like me. Are you sick? Is that it?"

"Yes," said Cotton, nodding furiously. "I-I don't feel so good." And as his knees suddenly failed him, he dropped down in his chair.

Ebony immediately pounced on him, pinning him down by placing both hands on the arms of the chair and bringing her face within inches of his. "You can't do this to Ebony, Cotton. Ebony won't be dumped by text. In fact Ebony won't be dumped, period. It's not done." And as she gazed deeply into his eyes, she sensed something was seriously wrong here. Usually when she was up close and personal with the man like this, the animal magnetism that had brought them together and caused electricity to crackle like wildfire, invariably made him drag her mouth to his and consume her in an explosion of heat.

But not now. She didn't feel a thing. The man was as passionate as a wet blanket.

She frowned at her former lover—the man who had set her world alight from the moment they first met at a Met Gala after-party. "Something isn't right," she determined. She pulled back, studying the wet blanket. "Something isn't right at all," she concluded.

She glanced to the lawyer, who seemed to have lost his tongue—a rare occurrence.

"This isn't over, Cotton!" she shouted as she retreated and walked out. "You haven't seen the last of me!"

And as she slammed the door, she wondered what the hell was going on.

🐾

Tobias stared after the woman, and winced as she slammed the door. The moment she was gone, Eric Blandine gave him a typically insipid look. "Do you think she knows?" he asked.

Tobias rubbed his chin thoughtfully. "I don't know. But she suspects something, that's for sure."

"Maybe you should have told her the truth?" Eric suggested.

"And have her run to the first reporter to spill the story? No way."

"What if she runs to the nearest reporter now?"

"She won't. She can't be sure that you're not Cotton."

Eric directed a dreamy look at the closed door. "What a woman," he sighed. Ebony's perfume still hung in the air, and Tobias had to admit it was as intoxicating as the lady herself.

But then he steeled himself. "This is exactly the kind of thing we have to avoid at all cost. If Ebony finds out, we're sunk—and that means this entire operation is sunk. And if the operation is a bust, Karat Group is dead meat."

"So what do suggest, Mr. Pushman?"

"I suggest that we tighten security. First that fracas at Town Hall, and now this?" He slammed the palm of his hand with his fist. "It's exactly this kind of thing we can't afford."

"She looked very upset," Eric mused. "I think she must love Cotton a great deal."

"That's not love," the lawyer scoffed. "It's lust."

"Lust," said Eric with a sigh. It was obvious he didn't know the meaning of the word. Then again, Tobias had seen Eric's wife. Not exactly a woman who inspired the kind of torrid emotion that Ebony Pilay seemed to inspire in the men she dated. "She's certainly something else," Eric concluded.

"Whatever she is," the lawyer concluded, his jaw working, "Miss Pilay is a problem."

That night, Ebony was gazing out of the window of the loft she inhabited. A glass of Chardonnay in her hand, her mind was filled with images of Cotton. Even though Ebony prided herself never to fall in love with the men she dated, she had to admit that Cotton had gotten under her skin. She wouldn't go so far as to say she'd fallen for the guy, but he was certainly a hard man to forget.

He was also the first man who'd ever dumped her.

She took a sip from the wine and savored it on her tongue. It brought back sweet memories of their first date. She'd only gone out with Cotton because a mutual friend had set them up, not expecting them to hit it off. But they had. In fact they hadn't even finished their meal. The night had ended with her in his arms in some hotel room near the restaurant, and they'd experienced one of those whirlwind romances you always hear so much about but which only seem to happen to people in the movies or on TV.

Cotton had taken her breath away, and frankly she'd already started allowing herself to think that he just might be the one.

And now this.

And as she thought back to that afternoon, suddenly a thought occurred to her. Was it possible that Cotton's entourage had drugged him? Or hypnotized him? He certainly hadn't seemed like himself. More like a watered-down version of the man she'd come to know so intimately she felt she knew him better than he knew himself.

And whoever the man she met was, it sure as hell wasn't Cotton.

Suddenly she thought she heard something—a noise that seemed to come from the entrance to the flat. And as she glanced over, suddenly a tiny sliver of fear struck her.

If these people could make Cotton disappear, what else were they capable of?

🐾

Eric Blandine had had an eventful day. He'd been doused with fake blood, accosted by the woman he had supposedly dumped, and so when he'd received the invitation, he'd figured it was just one more hurdle on the road to making this assignment a success.

For make no mistake: Eric might be the meekest, kindest man on the planet, but he was also determined to make a go at playing Cotton Karat. Even though he loved his job, it hadn't escaped his attention that here was the opportunity of a lifetime: the opportunity to make a great deal of money.

He could buy a house in the suburbs. He could get a decent car. He could take Maisie on the kind of holiday she deserved, instead of taking her camping again. In other words: if he played his cards right, this unusual request could completely turn their life around.

He entered the barn where the ducks were kept and wondered why they were meeting here. It's not as if he didn't have a perfectly nice condo where they could meet.

The odor of the ducks filled his nostrils and he grimaced. All around him, there was a kind of soft quacking, produced by the thousands of ducks gathered in the barn. Subdued light filtered in through grimy windows, and since he was afraid to make his presence known, and hadn't brought his phone or a flashlight, his well-shod right foot suddenly trod in something soft and squishy that he instantly knew was duck dung.

Yuck.

Sidestepping the first turd, he stepped in another turd with his other foot, to even things out.

Double yuck.

One nice thing about being Cotton were the fine clothes the man wore. He'd been granted access to Cotton's wardrobe, and he had to admit that whatever his faults were, the guy had taste. He checked his expensive watch and frowned when he noted the time.

"Where is—" he started to mutter, when suddenly he heard the sound of a footfall behind him. But when he whirled around to face the person, suddenly pain shot through the back of his head, a pain so sharp and unexpected that he cried out in agony.

And as he sank down to his knees, the last thought that passed through his mind was that now his five-thousand-dollar Tom Ford pants were going to be ruined, too.

CHAPTER 8

I woke up early again the next morning. Once again a loud scream tore me from a pleasant dream about a soft couch and a favorite blanket.

"Dooley!" Odelia yelled, and immediately I was wide awake.

I searched around, fearing the worst, but when my gaze encountered my friend's, and he looked back at me guiltily but very obviously alive and well, I let out a sigh of relief.

"Why!" Odelia cried. "Just tell me why!!!"

I frowned when I took in the scene. On Odelia's pillow this time no mouse, thank God. But when I looked closer, I saw that a tiny feathered thing had found its way thither. I had to really approach to discover what the little present was that Dooley had picked out for our human.

It was a bird. A tiny bird, but still a bird.

"I-I found it lying outside," Dooley explained timidly. "And I thought you'd enjoy the present."

"What is it?" asked Chase, yawning. Then he frowned. "Is that… a bird?"

"It is!" Odelia said. She was sitting bolt upright in bed and had folded her arms across her chest and was giving Dooley a look that brooked no contest. "Well? I'm waiting for an explanation."

"It's my USP!" Dooley said, a little lamely, I thought.

"Your what?"

"My USP. Max is the brains of this family, Brutus the brawn, Harriet the beauty, and I like to bring you little presents. It's what cats do," he added helplessly. "It's what I do."

"Well, I want you stop doing it, Dooley. I want you to stop bringing me little presents in the morning, especially if they consist of dead mice and dead birds!"

"Did Dooley kill a bird?" asked Chase with a note of concern to his voice.

"I didn't kill it," said Dooley. "It was already dead."

A worm now came poking its head to the surface of the dead bird's chest and both Odelia and Chase cried out in horror. It wasn't unlike that chestburster scene in *Alien*, only on a much smaller scale, of course.

"Looks like this bird has been dead a couple of days," Chase remarked dryly.

"Just get rid of it, will you?" said his wife.

"Want me to bury it, like I buried the mouse?"

"Yes, please do!" said Odelia, sounding out of sorts.

Then again, it probably isn't a pleasant sensation to find a dead bird on your pillow first thing in the morning.

"I thought you'd enjoy the present," said Dooley dejectedly.

"Well, I don't," said Odelia in a voice that brooked no contest.

And as we watched, the whole ritual started anew: after Chase had found a box appropriate for the mortal remains of the bird to be buried in, Odelia tore off the cover of her pillow, then tore off the cover of the duvet, and finally shoved covers and pillow and duvet into the washing machine, giving the knob a vicious twist as she did.

"Looks like that didn't hit the spot," said Dooley finally.

"No, it clearly did not," I agreed with him.

"Well, I'll just have to keep looking for my USP."

"No, Dooley, you don't," I said, but the mulish look on his face told me that I could argue until the cows came home, it was no good. He was going to look for his USP if it killed him. Or us. Then again, dead mice and birds probably aren't a health hazard. Or are they?

Moments later we were downstairs in the living room, chillaxing on the couch and keeping an eye on our humans as they got ready to start their working day. All of a sudden the doorbell chimed, and moments later Uncle Alec walked in. Odelia's uncle drops by so often Odelia has given him a key to the place. But like the nice guy he is, he rings first.

"Bad news, people," said the Chief as he ambled up. "There's been…" He sniffed the air. "Is that… bacon?"

"Yeah, want some?" asked Chase. He had donned an apron and was presiding over the stove, cooking up strips of bacon for himself and Odelia.

"Don't mind if I do," said Uncle Alec as he graced a kitchen stool with his bulk. "Charlene has gotten it into her nut that we're going to be vegetarians from now on," he explained. "And frankly it's driving me to despair."

"She must have been talking to Vesta," said Chase with a grin.

"Don't get me started on my ma," said the Chief, holding up his hand. "Did you know she was arrested yesterday for staging a protest against some foie gras guy?"

"Yeah, I heard about that."

"I had her released the moment I found out, of course. Otherwise I'd never hear the end of it."

"Did the foie gras guy file a complaint?"

"Well, that's just the thing. He's been murdered."

"Murdered!" said Chase, the wooden spoon hovering over the pan. "What do you mean, murdered?"

"Just what I'm telling you. Cotton Karat has been found murdered this morning. So you and Odelia better get out there ASAP and see what's going on. Meanwhile I'll take care of these for you," he added, sticking his fork into a glistening strip of bacon.

"Out there where?" asked Chase.

"Duck farm," said the Chief, tucking into his bacon with visible relish. "And get this, his liver has been removed."

Chase gulped at this. "His liver was removed?"

"Uh-huh," said Uncle Alec, chomping his meaty treat with unabashed delight. "Cut out of his body with a carving knife."

"Is that what killed him?"

Uncle Alec shrugged. "Guess so. I'm not a doctor, but I'd say it's probably tough to survive your liver being removed with a carving knife. Got any more of this stuff?"

Odelia had also arrived downstairs, and as the Chief filled her in on what had happened with Mr. Karat, it was obvious that contrary to Uncle Alec, neither Odelia or Chase had any desire to have breakfast after the gruesome details of the murder had been placed before him. The upshot was that the Chief got to eat their portions of bacon, too.

I guess when you're an involuntary vegetarian, it's all about those silver linings.

CHAPTER 9

It was our first murder case in a while, and obviously the killer hadn't stinted on the gore. When we arrived, the dead man was lying on his back in what appeared to be a pile of duck muck. Which wasn't all that surprising since this was, after all, a duck farm.

Abe Cornwall, the county coroner, sat hunched down over the corpse, and was scratching his head with an air of bewilderment. He looked up when we arrived.

"He seems to be missing his liver," said the frizzy-haired coroner.

"Yeah, the Chief intimated as much," said Chase.

"Oh, he did, did he?" said Abe as he got to his feet with some effort and a certain creaking of the joints. "Well, if it's true that the killer took the man's liver, I think I've just solved the murder for you." He spread his arms. "Must be Hannibal Lecter, in need of a liver enjoyed with some fava beans and a nice Chianti."

And chuckling unreservedly at his own little joke, he tore off his plastic gloves.

"So is that what killed him, you think?" asked Odelia,

ignoring the gallows humor.

"I'm not sure," said Abe, fingering his fleshy chin. "He's got a nasty bruise on the back of his head and his throat is slightly engorged."

"Knocked unconscious, then strangled?"

"No, not strangled. More as if... someone forced something down his throat. Though I doubt that's what killed him. I didn't find any other obvious injuries. No stab wounds or contusions. No defensive wounds on hands or arms. Nothing underneath his fingernails. In fact he appears to have been in excellent health before he lost one of his vital organs."

"Did you find the liver?" asked Chase, glancing around.

"Not yet," Abe said. "But if it really was Hannibal Lecter, I wouldn't, would I?"

"Do you have a time of death for me, Abe?" asked Chase a little curtly.

"Between ten and midnight, I'd say. And before you ask: judging from the copious amounts of blood and lividity he was killed right here on the spot. Killed and gutted."

"Murder weapon?"

"I'll go out on a limb here and say that you're looking for a serrated knife. Long, thin blade if I'm correct. Though I'll know more once I've had him on my slab." He grinned and stalked off, but not before adding, "You can expect my report on your desk, Kingsleys!"

"It's the same man who received that medal yesterday," said Dooley as we studied the dead man. "The one who got all of that fake blood thrown over him."

"Yeah, he didn't get to enjoy his medal for very long," I said.

"Do you think it was an accident?"

"I doubt it, Dooley. People don't accidentally lose their livers."

"You mean it couldn't accidentally have fallen out?"

"No, as far as I know a liver is firmly attached to a person's body."

"Oh."

"I wonder what he was doing out here," said Chase as he took in the grisly scene.

A uniformed police officer had walked up and tapped his head with his index finger as a sign of respect. "Dead man is a Cotton Karat, sir. Main client of this farm."

"Karat was a client of this duck farm?"

"Yes, sir. This place right here is where they produce the famous Karat foie gras. Best liver pâté in town, apparently, though I've never tasted it. Definitely the most expensive."

"Who found the body?"

"That would be a Merle Poltorak. He's the owner, sir. Arrived for work this morning and came upon the dead body of Mr. Karat here. Says he recognized him immediately."

"Well, he would, wouldn't he, if Karat was his main customer."

"What do you want us to do, sir?" asked the officer.

"Talk to the neighbors. Find out if they saw anything. Did you find Karat's car?"

"Yes, sir. It's parked out front."

"Check the GPS. See where he arrived from. Oh, and did you find his phone?"

"Yes, sir," said the copper, and handed Chase a plastic evidence bag containing a phone.

"Do you think this is connected with yesterday's incident?" asked Odelia once the officer had left to advise the rest of the team.

"The protest in front of Town Hall? It might be. They seemed a pretty determined bunch. Protesting against animal cruelty, were they?"

Odelia nodded. "Especially the process used to produce

foie gras."

"Foie gras," said Chase musingly. "Isn't that French for fatty liver?"

"There must be a connection," said Odelia. "We're in a duck farm, where foie gras was produced, and the farm's main client just lost his liver and had something forced down his throat." When Chase gave her an uncomprehending look, she added, "Foie gras is produced by force-feeding ducks or geese in a process called gavage. Basically they stick a tube down their throats, straight into their stomach. The treatment engorges the liver to unnatural proportions, which is then harvested and sold as a delicacy." She made a face. "It's a particularly cruel practice that's been banned in several countries."

"I see," said Chase as he surreptitiously touched his own throat.

"Poor ducks," said Dooley. "Being fed is nice, but being force-fed doesn't sound like a lot of fun."

"No, it certainly doesn't," I agreed. We glanced over to the ducks quacking away nearby, and decided to wander over and ask them if they saw anything last night.

The first duck we met looked a little swollen, as if his meal hadn't agreed with him. And of course I shouldn't wonder, if it was being forced down his gullet with a metal tube.

"Hiya, fella," I said in as pleasant a voice as I could muster. "How's things?"

"Not well," he said, sounding as if his food might come up at any moment. "In fact I feel a little peaky today. Must be the…" He burped a squelchy sort of burp. "… the weather."

"Yeah, must be," I said quietly. "So did you notice this guy arriving last night?"

"What guy?" asked the duck, who stared at us, a little cross-eyed I now saw.

"The guy who was found dead out there this morning."

"A dead guy? What dead guy?"

"Cotton Karat. He was killed sometime last night, right in front of your stall."

The duck thought for a moment, then finally his face cleared. "So that's what it was. I thought I heard some kind of fracas. I just figured it was humans doing human stuff, you know."

"Did you see what happened by any chance?"

He shrugged. "Not really. I like to keep myself to myself. Think it's rude to pry."

"What's your name, Mr. Duck?" asked Dooley.

"Fred," said the duck with a vague sort of smile.

"I'm Dooley," said Dooley. "And this is my friend Max. We're detectives."

"Detectives, huh? And what are you detecting?"

"The murder of Cotton Karat," said Dooley helpfully.

"Oh, right."

"So you didn't hear anything?" I asked. "Some kind of argument, maybe?"

"I did hear a scream. Very high, girly sort of scream."

"But you didn't think to take a look who it was that screamed?"

"Some human, I guess. I mean, who cares, right? They're always up to something, humans are. Strange breed, if you ask me. A little cruel and not very nice to us ducks."

"You didn't see one person stabbing another person?"

"I did take a quick peek, if that's what you mean."

"And?" I asked, anticipation making me a little breathless.

"One human was lying on the floor for some reason, and another was bent over them, doing something with a knife."

"Did you get a good look at the person?"

"Oh, sure."

"And?" I urged.

"It was a human," said the duck.

"I know it was a human," I said, trying to keep the exasperation out of my voice. "But what did this human look like is what I'd like to know."

The duck shrugged again. "They all look the same to me, humans do. If you've seen one, you've seen them all."

I suppressed the urge to scream. "Was this person a man or a woman? Tall or short? Fair-haired or dark-haired? It's very important, Fred, to get a detailed description."

The duck thought for a moment, then finally shook his head. "Nope," he said. "I'm drawing a complete blank here. Like I said, all humans look the same to me."

Now I did let out a groan of despair, but it was wasted on the duck, who simply gave me a sort of blank look, then smiled and said, "We're in the same boat, aren't we, cat?"

"What do you mean?" I asked.

He thrust out his rather bulging belly. "You're being groomed to have your liver removed too, aren't you? Though you look as if you're almost ready for harvesting."

Dooley suppressed a giggle at this, even as I threw the duck a dark look. It wasn't helpful, of course, since he was obviously a valuable witness. "Look, if something springs to mind about what happened last night, please let us know." I would have given him my card, but since cats don't carry cards, or smartphones, that wasn't really an option.

We returned to the scene of the crime, and I must confess I found it baffling that a murder could have been committed in the presence of a barn full of ducks, and apparently no one had seen anything. But maybe Fred was right. Maybe for them all humans did look alike. To most humans all ducks look alike, too, of course.

And we'd just joined Chase and Odelia, when the police officer returned and said, "A man is here to see you, sir. He says it's urgent."

"What man?" asked Chase, who'd been crouching over the body, taking a closer look.

"He says he's Cotton Karat's lawyer? A Tobias Pushman."

Moments later, we all stood outside with Mr. Pushman, who I remembered from the day before, when he'd been accompanying Mr. Karat to Town Hall. He looked as slick and well-dressed as yesterday, only his demeanor was more subdued, which was hardly surprising, considering he'd just lost his client.

"What I'm going to tell you has to stay between us," the lawyer urged Chase and Odelia.

"I'm sorry, sir," said Chase. "But I can't make that promise."

The lawyer thought for a moment, then decided to take his chances.

"That man in there? The man who died? His name isn't Cotton Karat."

Chase frowned. "And I have it on good authority that it is."

The lawyer sized Chase up for a moment, as if wondering if it was a good idea to take the detective into his confidence. "Cotton Karat is holed up in a rehab clinic right now, kicking a nasty addiction. I just spoke to him on the phone and he's alive and well."

Chase and Odelia shared a look of confusion. "So who is the dead man?" asked Chase.

"His name is Eric Blandine, and he was standing in for Cotton while he's staying at the clinic. You see, it was imperative that people thought it was business as usual at the Karat Group, in light of certain recent events that involved Cotton displaying behavior that reflected badly on the group."

"You mean the shareholders' meeting where he was drooling all over that model?"

The lawyer winced. "You can understand how a drop of fifty percent in share price had us all on the ropes. So it was decided that Cotton would take a step back, until he got his life back on track. In the meantime we asked Blandine to step in. And he did a great job."

"Are you telling us that it wasn't Cotton Karat who received that award yesterday?" asked Odelia. "But Eric Blandine?"

The lawyer nodded. "That's exactly what I'm saying."

"I thought he acted a little out of character," said Odelia.

"Eric was still learning the ropes. It was early days. But with a little help from me and Cotton's family, he was getting there." He dragged a hand through his perfect coiffure. "And now this," he said, gesturing to the barn.

"Do you have any idea who might have killed Mr. Jardine?" asked Chase.

"Blandine. And yes, I have a pretty good idea," said Tobias Pushman, his expression hardening. He reached into his car and came away with a sizable tin of foie gras. "This arrived at the office this morning."

"Foie gras?" asked Chase, staring at the tin.

"Not exactly," said Mr. Pushman, and opened the tin.

Judging from the horrified expressions on Chase and Odelia's faces, I understood it wasn't the delicacy that had made the Karat Group famous that was in that tin. But it was only when Odelia lowered the tin so Dooley and I could take a sniff that I understood.

The tin contained a perfectly preserved, gleamingly fresh human organ.

And if I wasn't mistaken, it was in fact Eric Blandine's liver.

CHAPTER 10

"There was also a message," said Tobias Pushman as he handed an envelope to Chase.

Odelia had quickly closed the tin and had put it in an evidence bag her husband had supplied. She and Chase now read the message the envelope contained.

Odelia read out loud for our benefit, "'The ducks will have their revenge! This is your first warning! Stop the atrocity or more people will die! Foie gras is murder! Ducks are people, too!'" She looked up. "Sounds a lot like the animal rights activists we saw yesterday."

"They like their exclamation marks, don't they, Max?" said Dooley, who'd listened with bated breath, just like I had.

"Activists in general aren't known for their subtlety," I said. "They like bold statements, and bold statements seem to include a lot of exclamation marks."

"Look at this," said Tobias as he pointed to the envelope.

Chase and Odelia squinted as they took in what looked like a symbol printed on the envelope. "DLF," Odelia finally read, and looked up at her husband. "It's the Duck Liberation Front. The group my gran and Scarlett joined."

"Wait, your grandmother is part of the group that killed Mr. Blandine?" asked Tobias.

"I'm sure she wasn't aware they're as radical as this," Odelia assured the lawyer.

"So this envelope arrived with the tin?" asked Chase.

Tobias nodded. "Was on Cotton's desk when I arrived at the office this morning."

"We better have it checked against Mr. Blandine," said Odelia. "But as far as I can tell—though I'm not an expert on human livers, obviously—this could very well be the murdered man's liver."

"In which case this Duck Liberation Front have just turned to murder as a way of protesting against foie gras," Chase concluded.

"Do you have any idea what Blandine was doing here last night?" asked Odelia.

"None. He certainly didn't advise me of his plans."

"When was the last time you saw him?"

"Yesterday at six. We left the office together. I went home, and I assumed he was going home, too."

"Where was home for Mr. Blandine while he was playing the part of Cotton Karat?" asked Chase.

"We'd set him up at Cotton's place for the time being. It was important that he looked the part, so we'd instructed him on the kind of clothes Cotton likes to wear, Cotton's hairstylist had given him a haircut, but otherwise we'd told Blandine to keep a low profile. He wasn't to go out to restaurants or socialize if he could avoid it. In fact we'd cleared his schedule as much as we could. The awards thing yesterday was something we couldn't get out of, unfortunately, but otherwise we were working to limit Blandine's exposure to an absolute minimum." He sighed. "Which is why I'm surprised he came here last night."

"Didn't he have security?"

"Of course. He had two bodyguards assigned to him at all times."

"So what happened?"

Tobias looked sheepish. "He gave them the slip. Said he'd gone to bed, but he must have snuck out through the bedroom window and taken off. They only found out this morning, when the maid came to open his bedroom curtains and discovered him gone."

Chase nodded, and studied Blandine's phone through the clear plastic of the evidence bag. "He must have received a message to meet him here at some point. A message from a person he thought he could trust. And walked straight into a trap."

"Well, it wasn't me," said Tobias, looking alarmed. "I had nothing to gain from Blandine's death. On the contrary. If the Karat Group goes belly-up I'm out of a job. Not to mention my stock options will be reduced to zero."

"Nevertheless I have to ask, Mr. Pushman. Where were you last night between ten and midnight?"

"I told you. I left the office at six and went home. I worked out at my home gym for an hour, then had dinner and spent the rest of the evening figuring out ways and means to further clear Blandine's schedule so we could pull off Cotton's big disappearance trick."

"Can anyone vouch for you?"

Tobias shook his head. "I live alone. But why would I kill Blandine? It makes no sense."

Chase grunted something, but I think we could all see that the lawyer had a point. Why would he go out and murder Eric Blandine? He had absolutely no reason to.

Which brought us right back to the Duck Liberation Front.

The next person to talk to was of course the poor guy who'd found the body. Merle Poltorak looked as distressed as anyone would be if the first thing they saw when they arrived for work were the murdered remains of their biggest client. Merle might be used to murdering ducks on a regular basis, but clearly the sight of Eric Blandine's corpse had affected him greatly. His weather-beaten face was quite pale and drawn.

"When exactly did you come upon the body of the dead man, Mr. Poltorak?" asked Chase.

"Seven o'clock," said Merle, rubbing a stubbled cheek. "I'd mucked out the big barn and was going to start on the smaller one when I practically stumbled over him. I knew he was dead the minute I laid eyes on him."

"Did you recognize him as Mr. Karat?"

Merle nodded. "I'd never met Cotton in person, but I've seen his picture plenty. It was him, all right. So I called the cops, and ten minutes later they were all over the place."

"Were you here last night, Merle?" asked Odelia.

"I was, until about eight. Then I went home."

"And where is home for you?"

"Right next door. The big farmhouse. Can't miss it when you drive up from the direction of town. I live there with Mrs. Poltorak and our four little ones."

"Four kids!" Dooley cried. "Did you hear that, Max? That man has four kids!"

"Must be a lively household," I commented. "Though it's a big farmhouse, so plenty of space."

"What if Odelia and Chase have four kids, Max! It's going to get very crowded!"

"I very much doubt whether they'll have four," I said. "Besides, if they do, they'll simply have to move, won't they? The house will be too small."

"But I don't want to move, Max! I like where we live!"

"Let's not worry about that now, shall we? Odelia is having one baby. One."

"What if it's quadruplets? Or quintuplets? Or sextuplets!"

"I very much doubt that Odelia is having more than one. We would have noticed."

He stared at Odelia very hard. "I see it now, Max."

"See what?"

"The bump!"

And he was right. Odelia was starting to show, which wasn't unusual, since she had been pregnant for a couple of weeks now.

"I'll bet it's septuplets or even octuplets," Dooley said morosely. "And no amount of dead mice or birds will make Odelia take any notice of me once those eight babies arrive."

"Oh, Dooley," I sighed. "Let's just focus on the case for now, shall we?"

"So what do you do here, exactly, Mr. Poltorak?" asked Chase.

"We raise ducks for slaughter," said Merle.

"And produce foie gras, right?" asked Odelia.

"Best foie gras in the county. Maybe even the country."

"Are you the sole producer of foie gras for the Karat Group?"

"That's right. We've always produced foie gras, though not exclusively for Karat. That changed about ten years ago. Since then we've only worked for the Karats. First Diedrich, and now Cotton. Though I have to admit that Diedrich was a much better boss than Cotton. Cotton is a little too wild for my taste, if you know what I mean."

"With his predilection for supermodels, you mean?" asked Chase.

"Yeah, that and his fondness for fast cars. One of these days he's going to get himself killed, I always said, and now it looks as if someone else has done him in."

"Do you have some kind of security in place at the farm?"

"Not really. Who wants to steal ducks? It's not exactly gold or diamonds."

"Do you have any idea who might have done this to him?" asked Odelia.

"Must be those animal rights nutters," said Merle. "They picketed outside the farm only last week, even threw a bucket of paint on my truck. And they threw a bucket of paint on Cotton yesterday at Town Hall. Though what I can't figure is what he was doing here in the middle of the night. He's never set foot on the farm before."

"What do you think will happen now?"

"I have no idea. Looks like the Karats ran out of people to run the business."

"Doesn't Cotton have a brother?"

"He does, but he's not interested in running the company. Or at least that's what I've heard." He held up his hands. "Honestly I don't care. I'm in charge of this here duck farm, that's all. What the Karats won't do is take away their business. We make them way too much money. Karat Foie Gras is pure gold. And Cotton's death won't change that."

CHAPTER 11

"I don't understand, Max," said Dooley. "What did Odelia mean when she asked if Cotton had a brother? Cotton isn't dead. Of course he'll return now and take over from poor Mr. Blandine again."

"It's not that simple," I said. "The whole point for Eric Blandine to step in was to whisk Cotton out of the limelight for a while, until this whole hubbub about his lurid ways had died down. The company stock took a big hit with that disastrous shareholders' meeting, and if it came out that he was being treated for sex addiction and that his replacement was murdered in his absence, it would probably hit the stock even harder, and send it plummeting into the basement, trading at cents on the dollar. It might spell the end."

"I don't think so. I think people will be so happy that Cotton didn't die, the stock will go up."

But since it wasn't up to us to figure out the right strategy to handle this murder from a business perspective, I didn't want to spend valuable time thinking up possible strategies. That was for the Karat Group's PR department and the company principals.

In the meantime, we were heading to the home of Eric Blandine's wife to give her the bad news. Never a pleasant task, but nevertheless one that has to be done.

Odelia had been on the phone and now disconnected. "Looks like Blandine didn't get contacted through his phone," she said. "The tech department didn't find any messages setting up last night's meeting, and no phone calls either."

"Email, maybe?"

"No email either, as far as they can tell. They're still looking at his laptop, though, so maybe they'll have better luck there."

"He was using his own mobile, not Cotton's?"

"No, he still had his own mobile. All calls for Cotton were forwarded to Tobias Pushman for the time being, who was acting like a shield." She absentmindedly chewed her fingernail. "So how did they get in touch with Blandine? And how did they manage to get him out there in the middle of the night?"

"Odelia?" asked Dooley, scooting forward a little on the backseat.

"Mh?"

"If you're having octuplets you would tell us, right?"

Odelia laughed at this. "Octuplets! I hope not!"

Chase glanced over to his wife. "Who's having octuplets?"

"Me! According to Dooley, at least."

"Imagine having eight," Chase grunted, gripping the steering wheel a little tighter.

Odelia darted an amused look at her hubby. "Oh, I don't know. I think it would be a lot of fun. A house filled with joy and laughter and all that."

"But babe—eight!" Chase cried, going white around the nostrils.

"So? I was an only child, and so were you, so don't tell me

you never thought of having a little brother or sister when you were growing up?"

"I did, but not eight!"

"I think it'll be fun."

"Fun!"

"Oh, relax, sourpuss! I'm not having eight babies."

Chase blew out a sigh of intense relief. "Oh, phew."

"But I'm not ruling out septuplets."

"Septuplets!" Chase and Dooley cried out in unison. "No way!"

"Okay, fine! How about just the one then?"

"One I can handle," said Dooley. "Though only barely."

"One is fine," Chase grunted. "Or even two or three."

"Well, it's just the one," said Odelia, sinking lower in her seat and putting her feet up on the dash.

"Babe, don't do that," said Chase. "And make sure that seatbelt's securely fastened."

"Okay, grandma," said Odelia with a grin, but she removed her feet from the dash and sat up straighter. "Though you can drive the legal limit, you know."

She was right. For some reason we were crawling along the road, with at least a dozen cars behind us, a few drivers leaning on their horns.

"It's important to be safe," Chase pointed out. "Road safety is no laughing matter."

"I know, babe," said Odelia, rubbing the cop's arm affectionately. "But at this rate we'll arrive there next week. And we still have lots of people to see, you know. Or don't you want us to nab this nasty killer?"

"Oh, all right," said Chase, and sped up a smidgen—but only a smidgen.

I glanced over and saw that Dooley was beaming for some reason. "Why are you so happy all of a sudden?" I asked.

"One baby, Max," he whispered. "She's only having one baby!"

I smiled. "I know."

"One baby I can handle. I think." His face clouded a little. "Or maybe not."

"Of course we can handle one baby," I said. "Besides, babies aren't dangerous, you know. They're not live grenades that can go off any second."

"Says you," he said, and his frown had returned. I had the impression that as long as that baby hadn't been born, my friend would continue to fret and worry. Then again, Dooley always frets and worries. If it's not about babies, it's about the sky falling or some terrible disease laying waste to the entire family. He watches too much television, I guess.

We'd finally arrived at the home of Mr. and Mrs. Blandine, and we all got out. It was a modest little home on a quiet street. I wondered now how the Karats had discovered the likeness between Cotton and Eric, but I was sure the man's wife would tell us all about it.

Mrs. Blandine was a short, stocky woman with a bob of dark hair and a square face. She'd been crying, I saw, which meant that either she'd been peeling onions, or someone had already broken the news to her.

"I'm very sorry to say that I have some bad news for you about your husband, Mrs. Blandine," said Chase as we stood on the porch.

"I know!" the woman wailed. "He's dead, isn't he!"

"How did you…"

"We heard the news this morning," said a man, stepping to the fore. He looked very much like Cotton Karat, or indeed Eric Blandine, only there was more of him. Twice as much, actually, a lot of it centered around his waistline, and the rest evenly distributed across his face and neck. It was uncanny. As if Cotton Karat was donning a fat suit. "I'm Eric's brother Fabrizio," the man explained.

"How did you hear about what happened?" asked Chase as we stepped into the house.

"The company lawyer called," Fabrizio explained. "Tobias Pushman. Asked us to refrain from comment in case we heard it on the news. And reminded us that Eric signed a nondisclosure agreement which extended to his immediate family."

"They don't want us to talk to the media," said Mrs. Blandine, sniffling as she took a seat on a baggy couch and grabbed a handful of tissues from a box on the coffee table.

"I'm very sorry for your loss," said Chase.

"I'm going to sue them, you know," said the newly widowed woman. "They killed him!"

"We don't know that, Maisie," said Mr. Blandine, patting the woman's hand. He'd taken a seat next to her, and was playing the part of the consoling relative to perfection.

"Of course we do!" Maisie cried, lifting a teary face to her brother-in-law. "They asked him to pretend to be Cotton Karat and now those crazies killed him! This would never have happened if he hadn't listened to them."

"It wasn't as if he was in a position to refuse," said Fabrizio quietly.

"What do you mean?" asked Odelia.

"I mean they put a lot of pressure on my brother."

"They practically forced him," said Maisie. "Said that if he didn't do what they wanted they were going to have him fired. So he decided to play along. And then there were those stock options, of course."

"The stick and the carrot," said Fabrizio wryly. "First they threatened him, then they dangled stock options in front of his nose. Said that if the stock went up, he'd be on velvet."

"How much, if I may ask?" asked Chase.

"Ten," said Maisie. "At today's stock price that means five thousand, and if the stock went back up to a thousand, like it was before Cotton screwed up, ten thousand."

"How long was he going to have to pretend to be Cotton?"

Maisie shrugged. "Couple of weeks. A month, maybe. It all depended on how long it took Cotton to get his act together."

"Sex addiction," said Fabrizio tersely. "First time I heard of it."

"Oh, it's a thing," Maisie assured him. "Some Hollywood actors have it."

"I'll bet they do," Fabrizio grumbled. It was obvious he didn't have a high opinion of Cotton Karat.

"I noticed how Cotton's girlfriend Ebony Pilay wasn't at the award ceremony at Town Hall yesterday," said Odelia.

"They dumped her," said Maisie. "By text, if you please. She wasn't happy, I can tell you that. Came into the office and started screaming all kinds of abuse at my Eric. Poor sweetheart didn't know what to do. It's not his fault these people are inhuman. They told him they bought her off, but instead they told her to take a hike. She didn't take it well."

"Ebony came into the office yesterday?"

"She did. And she was furious. Wouldn't you be? A supermodel like her? Dumped by text? She was screaming bloody murder!" She then seemed to realize what she was saying, for she quickly glanced to her brother-in-law. "Not that I think she's capable of murder, mind you. But she definitely was very upset, and quite rightly so."

"It's that lawyer," said Fabrizio. "He cooked this all up."

"Not just the lawyer. Him and Diedrich are in this together."

"Cotton's dad set up this whole business with your husband?" asked Odelia.

"He most certainly did. Wants to protect the Karat Group's bottom line, doesn't he?"

"How did your husband get roped into this, Mrs. Blandine?" asked Chase.

"Eric has always been teased about his resemblance to Cotton. His colleagues all call him Goldie, for karat gold? And a couple of weeks ago there was a factory visit by the big brass. Though only Tobias showed up. Norm must have told him about Eric, cause a couple of days ago he was suddenly in Norm's office, along with Diedrich himself."

"Hold on—are you saying your husband worked for the Karat Group?"

"Yeah, in one of the group's warehouses. They've got plenty, spread out across the country. Eric's worked there for years. Hard work, but the pay isn't too bad. At least you have to give them that. They take care of their own. Not like some of those bloodsuckers."

I watched as she picked up her used tissue, and carefully tucked it away in a shoebox. When the others watched on, she said, with a touch of embarrassment, "I dry them and reuse them. Same for teabags. Did you know you can still get a decent pot of tea out of a teabag that's been used twice before? People these days throw away stuff too quickly."

"Maisie here is your true environmentalist," said Fabrizio warmly. "She's the queen of recycling."

"It's just a habit," said Maisie. "Drives Eric up the wall sometimes." Her face crumpled. "Oh, my poor Eric! Who would want to kill my sweet, sweet husband!"

"When did you last talk to Eric, Maisie?" asked Chase.

"Last night around eight. He called every night. That's when he told me about Ebony barging into his office yesterday, and also about that paint those terrible people threw on him, ruining a perfectly good suit. Though he assured me those spots were going to come out. Tobias had promised him they'd pay for the dry-cleaning."

"Did you notice anything out of the ordinary when you talked to him?" asked Odelia.

"You mean apart from the Pilay woman and those duck-loving freaks?"

"Yes, apart from that."

Maisie shook her head. "He sounded a little rattled, but wouldn't you be if you were attacked twice in one day, first with a bucket of paint and then by some furious model?"

"He didn't mention that he was planning to meet someone last night?"

"No, he didn't say anything about that. You mean he went out there to meet his killer?"

"He must have received a message or a phone call," said Chase. "Why else would he head down to a duck farm in the middle of the night?"

"He hadn't been there before?" asked Odelia.

"No, never. I've never even heard of that place."

"It's those duck lovers, isn't it?" said Fabrizio. "They probably kidnapped him and then killed him, mistaking him for that Cotton Karat." He gritted his teeth. "My brother should never have gone along with this crazy business. If he hadn't, he'd still be alive today."

At this, Maisie picked up one of the used tissues and loudly blew her nose in it.

She was right. You probably could use those more than once. Who knew?

"He wasn't kidnapped as far as we can tell," said Chase. "We found his car parked in front of the farm, so he must have driven there under his own steam."

"Maybe they took him there at gunpoint?" Fabrizio suggested. "Made him drive his own car?"

"I can promise you that we're looking into all of that," said Chase. "But for now, can you tell us where you both were last night between ten and midnight?"

Maisie and her brother-in-law shared a look of surprise. "You don't think we had anything to do with what happened to my husband, do you?" asked Maisie.

"Just a routine inquiry, I can assure you," said Odelia kindly.

"Well, I was right here," said Maisie. "After Eric called, I watched some television and went to bed."

"And you, Mr. Blandine?"

"Same. I mean, I watched TV and went to bed."

"Can anyone vouch for that?"

They both shook their heads.

"You're not married?" asked Chase.

"I was married, but my wife left me," said Fabrizio unhappily.

"Look, how is this important?" asked Maisie.

"We're trying to form a picture of your husband, Mrs. Blandine," said Odelia. "What he was like, what kind of life he led, the people he knew—everything we can find out."

"But isn't it obvious that he was killed because someone thought he was Cotton?"

"It's all right, Maisie," said Fabrizio. "My wife left me for her fitness instructor. He's about ten years younger than she is. This was five years ago. We never had kids, so that's why I was home alone last night, just like I've been home alone every night for the past five years. I hope that satisfies your curiosity?"

He was starting to get a little belligerent, which wasn't surprising. People whose relatives have just been killed don't enjoy answering a lot of questions probing into their personal lives, especially when those questions touch upon a sensitive topic.

"I hope you'll catch Eric's killer," said Maisie when she escorted us to the door. "And I hope you'll let us have his body as soon as possible. We have a funeral to arrange, after all." And with these words, she slammed the door shut.

"That was fun," said Chase as we returned to the car.

"It always is," Odelia said.

"At least Tobias didn't tell them about the removed liver," said Chase as he clicked his seatbelt into place. "Though at some point they will need to be told."

"Best they hear it from us," said Odelia, "and not the newspaper."

Which was ironic, since Odelia is a reporter, after all. Then again, she's not that kind of reporter—the kind that loves to dish out the most gruesome and gory details of a case, hoping to shock people and drive up circulation.

Just at that moment, a message came in on Chase's phone. He read it, a frown on his face. "Abe," he clarified. "Looks like Eric Blandine was stabbed to death. Single stab wound to the abdomen, his liver removed after the fact. Also, the liver that was sent to the office was indeed Blandine's." He shared a look with his wife. "Let's have a chat with the Duck Liberation Front."

CHAPTER 12

The person in charge of the Duck Liberation Front or DLF was a young woman named Lita Fiol. She worked behind the checkout at the Happy Bean, a shop that sells all manner of product that might appeal to your health-minded fellow man, and has a selection especially devoted to the vegetarian section of the population.

The Happy Bean wasn't exactly buzzing with life when we stepped into the store and listened to the happily clanging bell attached to the door. Only a single customer was present, and seemed to have a hard time deciding between various iterations of tofu.

Lita Fiol wasn't thrilled to see us, and with us of course I mean Chase, as a representative of the police department.

"I've talked to your people already," she said the moment Chase had produced his badge and so had Odelia. "And I've got nothing to add. The man got exactly what he deserved for murdering thousands upon thousands of innocent ducks. It was one bucket of paint, for crying out loud! Send me the bill for the dry cleaners and I'll happily pay it."

She was a petite sort of woman, dressed in an eclectic

assortment of clothes. I detected a tie-dye T-shirt in psychedelic colors, a black sleeveless shirt draped across it, a chain around her neck from which a small dreamcatcher dangled, and black leggings over white lace-up sneakers. Her hair was short and stylishly messy, and she wore plenty of black eyeliner and a nose piercing. All in all, I guess, she looked like your average teen, though she was probably in her early to mid-twenties.

"We're not here about the paint, Miss Fiol," said Chase.

"I'm afraid there's been a murder," Odelia explained.

The girl's eyes went wide. "A murder!"

"A man named Eric Blandine was murdered last night," said Chase. "He'd been hired by the Karat Group to replace Cotton Karat for the time being. The man you dumped paint on yesterday was in fact Mr. Blandine, and not Mr. Karat."

The girl blinked. "I don't understand."

"For reasons we won't go into, Blandine was hired to take Cotton's place."

"Mr. Blandine was murdered at a duck farm," said Odelia. "His liver was removed and placed in a foie gras tin, then delivered along with a message to his office this morning. The message was sent by the Duck Liberation Front." She showed the message on her phone, and Lita read it with blood creeping up her cheeks until they were both a bright crimson.

"Did you send this message, Miss Fiol?" asked Chase finally.

"No, of course not! Are you crazy? Send a man's liver to..." She blinked. "Wait a minute. Are you accusing me of murdering this guy and shipping his liver off to his office?"

"In light of the fact that you've been staging multiple protests against Mr. Karat and the foie gras his company produces, and after the protest yesterday at Town Hall, I don't think it's hard to imagine you or one of your members are behind this business."

She held up her hands in a gesture of defense. "Look, I admit I had a beef with the guy. But I would never murder him. I'm not a violent person, Detective Kingsley."

"She looked a little violent yesterday," Dooley commented.

"They all looked a little violent," I agreed. "Even Gran and Scarlett."

"Do you think Gran is behind this? Her and Scarlett?"

"I don't think so. Though it probably won't hurt to ask."

"Where were you last night between ten and midnight, Miss Fiol?" asked Chase.

She blinked. "Home. Alone."

"Is that right?"

"Yes, that's right," she said, taking a defiant stance.

"I'm going to need a list of all the members of the DLF."

"Impossible."

"We could get a warrant," said Odelia.

"And search your house," said Chase, "search this shop—get that list off your computer."

"You wouldn't dare."

"I don't think you understand the trouble you're in, Miss Fiol. A man has been brutally murdered, his liver removed as if he was a duck, and a message from your organization sent to his office claiming responsibility for the murder."

"But I didn't do it!" she cried.

Just then, the client who'd been perusing the tofu section approached the counter. It was an elderly lady who was holding up two packets of tofu. "Can you please tell me which one of these has chicken, miss?"

"I'll be with you shortly," said Lita with a strained smile. "After I've dealt with these people."

"Oh, all right," said the woman, and wandered off again.

"Look, I was at a DLF meeting last night, all right?" said Lita. "I didn't want to tell you, since some of our members don't appreciate it when their names and pictures are plastered all over the paper."

"So why do they join the protests?" asked Odelia, not unreasonably. "They must know they'll be photographed."

This had Lita stumped for a moment, then she rallied. "Not all of our members take part in our protests. Some of them prefer to work behind the scenes."

"Fine," said Chase. "I'm going to need the names and addresses of all the people who were present at your meeting."

"But..."

"What time did the meeting break up?"

"Eleven-ish."

"Plenty of time to drive down to Karat Farm and gut Mr. Blandine."

"No! I didn't leave the house again. My boyfriend can confirm that."

"What boyfriend? You just said you were home alone all night."

The girl emitted a resigned sigh. "He doesn't like to be dragged into DLF business."

"Name?" Chase demanded curtly, his pencil poised over his notepad.

"Tobias Pushman."

This caused a small measure of consternation, then Odelia asked, "Tobias Pushman as in the head of the Karat Group's legal department? That Tobias Pushman?"

Lita nodded. "We've been seeing each other for the last couple of months. We met at one of the DLF protests. I chucked a bucket of paint at him, and instead of sending me the dry-cleaning bill he dropped by the store to hand me his soiled suit. We got to talking, and for some strange reason we hit it off. We had lunch, then we had dinner, then we started dating. We haven't told anyone."

"I can't imagine why," said Chase.

"Please don't tell him I told you," she pleaded. "He's going to be in so much trouble if the Karats find out he's been dating their worst enemy."

"I wonder what they talk about when they're alone in bed," said Dooley.

"Ducks, probably," I said. "They're both in the duck business, after all."

"Yes, but she's trying to save ducks, and he's murdering them on an industrial scale."

"Or maybe they don't talk about ducks at all? Probably better to leave the topic unaddressed."

"Thank you for your time," said Chase. "And don't forget: I'm going to need that membership list on my desk by tonight, or else."

"But I've given you my alibi!"

"And don't think we won't check it," Chase warned her.

As we left the shop, we heard the old lady ask, "Which one of these has beef, miss?"

"There's no meat in tofu, all right! It's soy—just soy!"

"Soy? What kind of meat is that? Not pig, surely."

"Oh, my God!"

Clearly the best friend ducks ever had was under a great deal of strain.

CHAPTER 13

The main offices of the Karat Group looked like any other office building the world over: a bland block of glass and concrete, absolutely devoid of personality or individuality. In other words: a joyless mass created by an uninspired architect who, like most captains of industry, seemed to believe that in order to be productive, one must also be miserable.

Chase parked his car in the parking spot reserved for Cotton Karat himself, correctly assuming that the man wasn't in need of it right now, and we entered the soulless complex.

We were soon greeted in the lobby by Tobias Pushman, and I must say I found myself looking at the lawyer in an entirely different light.

"I really can't see him with Lita Fiol, Max," said Dooley. "They just don't seem to fit."

"No, they're worlds apart, that's for sure," I said. "Though you know what they say about opposites, Dooley."

"They're sworn enemies?"

"No, they attract, apparently."

"I don't see it, Max. I really don't."

Tobias led us into his former boss's office—though it was in actual fact his current boss's office, since his real boss was actually still alive. It was his fake boss who'd been murdered.

Eric's laptop had already been removed by the tech people, who'd also processed the office for possible clues as to the man's late-night meeting with his murderer.

"We interviewed Lita Fiol just now," said Chase, and I think we all watched the lawyer closely to see how he'd react. He didn't flinch. Not even a squint or a grimace.

"Cool customer," was Dooley's estimation of the man.

"Oh?" said Tobias. "Who is she?"

"You know very well who she is, Mr. Pushman."

A smile spread across the lawyer's face. "Of course. The Duck Liberation Front. So what did Miss Fiol have to say for herself?"

"She claims she couldn't have killed Mr. Blandine, since she was in bed with you at the time."

This time the lawyer did flinch. He even blanched, then tucked a finger between neck and collar and tugged. "Is that what she said?"

"Oh, yes."

"A case of opposites attract, Mr. Pushman?" asked Odelia with a fine smile.

The lawyer coughed into his fist, clearly buying himself some time.

"What do you talk about at night, I wonder," said Chase. "Ducks?"

"No, we avoid the topic," said Tobias, then sank down onto the edge of Cotton Karat's desk. He rubbed his face. "Look, I never asked for this, you know. It just happened. I still don't know why. Cruel twist of fate, maybe? And I've asked Lita a million times to stop badgering my employer. But she believes in her cause. And I can only admire her for it."

"What did you think when that box arrived with a letter from Lita's action group?"

"I was hoping she'd have an explanation for me," said Tobias. "Which is why I tried calling her this morning, but of course I couldn't reach her since she tends to switch off her phone when she's at work." He held up his hands. "Look, I know Lita. She's the ultimate nature lover. In that she would never harm anyone, man or beast."

"You're not covering for her, are you, sir?" asked Odelia.

"No, of course not!"

"Why did you say you were home alone last night?"

"Because I want to keep my relationship with Lita Fiol a secret, of course! Can you imagine what it would look like if people knew? The lawyer of one of the biggest foie gras producers in the country dating the leader of the Duck Liberation Front? It wouldn't look good, I can tell you that. Not for me, and not for her."

"Okay, so how do you explain the DLF connection?" asked Chase.

"I can't! That's what's so infuriating. Look, Lita is harmless, all right? Apart from a couple of dry-cleaning bills the extent of her actions are some bruised egos and maybe a raised awareness that the way this industry has been treating animals is something we need to look at."

"She's a big threat to your bottom line."

"She's not. No, really," he added when Chase quirked a skeptical brow. "We all know that we need to make sure that animals are treated in a more humane way, and I can assure you that the Karat Group is well aware of this, and that steps are being taken in that direction. In that sense Lita and I are both on the same side—absolutely. No, all I can think is that one of her members has decided to take matters into their own hands."

"Behind Lita's back?"

"Of course," Tobias agreed. "A lot of people have signed up recently. In fact Lita told me only yesterday about two members she felt were a little overzealous." He took out his phone. "I even wrote down their names. Ah, here they are. Vesta Muffin and Scarlett Canyon. They actually wanted to use real blood yesterday, instead of the usual red paint."

"We'll look into them, sir," said Chase, exchanging a look of amusement with Odelia. "Now can you take us to the person who received that tin containing Blandine's liver?"

Tobias nodded and picked up the phone on Mr. Karat's desk. A moment later, he hung up. "I've asked her to come up."

"Have you decided how to handle the death of Mr. Blandine?" asked Odelia.

"I've been in conference with Diedrich and the PR people all morning, and they seem to think that the best way is to be honest. Simply tell the truth and get it over with."

"I can imagine that's going to be a tough pill to swallow."

"Yeah, well, it can't be helped. Let's just hope people will understand. Ah, here she is."

While Chase and Odelia interviewed the person in charge of the mailroom, and tried to track down how exactly the package had arrived, when it had arrived, and which route it had traveled to finally arrive on Cotton Karat's desk, Dooley and I wandered off and inspected a potted plant nearby. I won't conceal that I was starting to get a little peckish. We'd been on the go all morning, without so much as a bathroom break, and frankly I'd hoped that these Karat people would have something edible in store for us.

Unfortunately they did not condone pets in the office, and therefore had no pet food to dispense either.

"I'm still wondering how Eric Blandine died," said Dooley as we hopped up onto a nice blue sofa and settled in for the duration. If we couldn't eat, at least we could nap.

"What do you mean? He was stabbed and his liver was removed, Dooley. The human body can't survive a harsh treatment like that."

"It's a liver, Max. Can't people survive without a liver?"

"No, they can't."

"But it's not a heart, or a pair of lungs. Now if his heart had been removed, or his lungs, I could understand, but a liver? I didn't even know humans had livers until this morning."

"What do you mean? Of course humans have livers. Just like we have livers."

"Are you sure?"

"Of course!"

"But why?"

"What do you mean, why?"

"I mean, what does it do? Why do we need it?"

"The liver helps with digestion, eliminates toxins, synthesizes proteins and hormones. It's a very, very important organ."

"I still think he could have survived a couple of hours without it. Which means he was probably poisoned. And we all know that poison is the murder weapon of choice for the female killer. Which means that Lita Fiol is the person we're looking for, Max."

"But she couldn't have done it, Dooley. She was with her boyfriend Tobias."

"So they did it together. Tobias was lured over to the dark side of duck activism, and so they both decided that Cotton had to die since he was in the duck-harming business."

"Tobias knew that Eric Blandine was replacing Cotton Karat. So why kill him?"

"To send a message, of course! Don't mess with the ducks! Of course Tobias didn't want to kill the real Cotton Karat, since that would mean his stock options would drop in value and also he'd be out of a job. But this Eric Blandine? No problem. So they decided to sacrifice the poor man as a victim of the cause."

"Oh, Dooley," I sighed. Looked like my friend didn't have all his ducks in a row.

CHAPTER 14

Before continuing their investigation, Odelia and Chase decided to take stock for a moment, and dropped by Odelia's office. It allowed Dooley and myself to finally enjoy half a bowl of kibble, and a visit to the litter box Odelia has installed in her office. And not a moment too soon, either, for I'd been wondering how much longer I could tell my bladder to behave!

It transpired that the package that arrived at the Karat Group offices had been hand-delivered sometime during the night or early morning. After a thorough reconstruction had been carried out, it was determined that the package had been found in the Karat Group mailbox by Laurence Grifka, the person in charge of the mailroom, who had personally placed it on a trolley destined for the upper floor.

She remembered so distinctly since it was the only package in the mailbox, since it was already there before the post arrived. Also, it had been tied up with string and looked like something either a child or the Unabomber had dreamed up.

Once the actual post had arrived, and had been sorted,

the trolley had started its ascent through the company, until it had finally arrived on the top floor, where Cotton Karat's personal secretary Opal Saryusz had taken reception of the package along with the rest of Cotton's mail, and had placed it on her boss's desk. Opal was one of the few people who knew that Cotton wasn't actually Cotton, since she knew the real man too well to be so easily deceived.

The last link in the chain had been Tobias, who had opened the package and made the gruesome discovery.

Which meant that we still had no idea who had delivered the package, since there were no CCTV cameras covering the mailbox, and the cameras that covered the parking lot hadn't picked up any strange activity last night or in the early part of the morning.

"Odd that Tobias and the woman who runs the duck group would be dating," said Odelia as she tucked into a cheese sandwich Chase had picked up from the deli around the corner. He himself had procured a ham sandwich, defying potential abuse from Gran and Scarlett.

"I think they make a cute couple," said Chase. "And who knows? Maybe they'll be able to make the foie gras industry more ethical."

He'd received Abe Cornwall's final report, which contained one gruesome detail we hadn't yet been made privy to. Apparently whoever killed Eric Blandine had shoved a pipe down the man's throat and poured the same mixture of corn and fat down his gullet that they used on the ducks to artificially fatten up their livers to unnatural proportions. The mixture had been found in the man's stomach as the last meal he digested.

And the tech people had finished examining Eric's laptop and phone and had found no trace of a message he'd received setting up his late-night meeting.

"It must be the duck people that did this," said Odelia. "If not Lita, then someone who's part of her outfit."

"Maybe we should talk to your grandmother. She's already part of this group. She might be able to tell us who are some of the more radical elements."

"According to Lita and Tobias she and Scarlett are the radical elements," said Odelia with a grin.

"Why am I not surprised," said the cop.

"So what's next?"

"We still have to talk to Ebony," said Chase, consulting his notebook. "And I just got confirmation from Tobias that he's managed to set up an interview with the man himself. Cotton Karat has carved out five minutes of his busy day for us."

"He's home?"

"Arriving home later today. The interview will take place at the clinic, though."

"That was a very short stay. So he's fully cured of his sex addiction, then?"

"I very much doubt it. But he's got a press conference at four."

"That sounds promising."

"If you're a reporter, sure. As a cop? Not so much. Though it might be interesting to keep a close eye on the room. If the killer thought he murdered Cotton, and now all of a sudden that same Cotton turns up alive and well, that must be a great blow."

"You think the killer will turn up at the press conference?" asked Odelia.

"Wouldn't you?"

Odelia nodded thoughtfully. "Why don't you talk to my uncle? Get a couple of cameras covering the room, and officers spread out to listen in on conversations, look at people texting on their phones. Maybe we'll pick up on something that way."

"Great idea, babe," said Chase, and took out his own phone. "Consider it done."

"We can also spread out, Odelia," I suggested. "We can ask Harriet and Brutus to join us. If we all cover a part of the room, we might be able to glean something important."

"Thanks, Max," said Odelia, giving me a pat on the head. "That would be great."

"Do you really think the killer will turn up?" asked Dooley.

"Who knows?" I said. "If Cotton was the intended victim, the killer might want to take another crack at him. And he'll definitely want to see for himself if the man is still alive."

"I hope they'll protect Cotton from now on," said Dooley. "If the killer tries again, they have to stop him before another man loses his liver." He frowned, then directed himself to our human. "Are you sure that a person actually needs their liver, Odelia? It doesn't sound like something important. I mean, people lose their appendix or even a kidney and it doesn't make a difference."

"Yes, Dooley," said Odelia with a patient smile. "People really do need their liver. It's a vital organ."

"Oh. Well, too bad."

"Tell that to Eric Blandine," I muttered, then devoured another helping of kibble. I had the distinct impression that today was going to be a long day.

CHAPTER 15

I'd just managed to strengthen the inner cat when Gran came storming into the office, followed by Scarlett and Harriet and Brutus. They all looked a little hot under the collar.

"What's all this I hear about you arresting the leading light in duck salvation?" Gran demanded heatedly.

"If you're referring to Lita Fiol, she's not under arrest at this moment," said Chase, not too bothered by this outburst as evidenced by the leisurely way he was scrolling on his phone. "She is, however, a person of interest in our investigation, that much is true."

"A person of interest! She's as white as the driven snow! The girl is a peach!"

"She's also the leader of the Duck Liberation Front, and as such the most likely suspect in our case," Chase pointed out, looking up from his phone and directing a warning glance at Gran and her cronies.

But if he thought a mere threatening look would silence Gran, he was sorely mistaken. Warning looks only serve to embolden that old lady. "She's a role model! A paragon of heroism. Setting an example for her generation! If not for her, ducks will continue to be slaughtered by the ravenous bloodlust of the common masses! You should give her a medal, and not that no-good, head butcher Cotton Karat."

"You do know that this head butcher of yours was himself butchered last night?" asked Odelia, lifting an eyebrow.

Gran's mouth opened and closed a few times. "Butchered? What are you talking about?"

"Cotton Karat, or at least the man who was pretending to be Cotton Karat, was murdered last night. Someone shoved a tube down his throat, forced duck food into his stomach, and then proceeded to cut out his liver. Suffice it to say the man did not survive the treatment."

"Did you say the man who was pretending to be Cotton?" asked Scarlett, the first to recover from the shock.

"Yeah, turns out Cotton is in a rehab clinic, trying to kick a sex addiction," Chase grunted. "So the guy they hired to replace him for the time being ended up being the one who was murdered. Though it's safe to say that it was actually Cotton they were after."

"So let me get this straight," said Gran. "The man the killer thought was Cotton Karat was murdered in a manner very similar to the way ducks are slaughtered?"

"That's exactly what happened," said Odelia, nodding. "Only his liver was subsequently removed and delivered to his office with a message from the Duck Liberation Front, announcing that this was only a first warning. So it looks as if your precious DLF is only getting started and more victims might follow this first one."

"Especially when they find out they got the wrong guy," Chase muttered.

"I don't buy this," said Gran. "My DLF would never do such a horrible thing."

"No, we're all peace-loving people," Scarlett chimed in. "We don't condone violence."

"Anyway, you can relax about Lita," said Odelia. "Turns out she has a solid alibi for the time of the murder. Which isn't to say that someone else in your group isn't the murderer."

"Speaking of which," said Chase, "now might be a good time to take a long, hard look at some of the other members, and find out who might be the person we're after." And to show them what he meant, he gave the twosome a long, hard look.

"Oh, no!" said Gran immediately. "You're not going to get us to spy on our own!"

"Vesta, maybe Chase has a point," said Scarlett. "If one of us is a killer, it's going to reflect very badly on the rest."

"But we're not police spies!"

"I thought that crime prevention was what the neighborhood watch did?" asked Chase finely.

It was clear that two powerful emotions wrestled in Gran's bosom: her allegiance to the duck cause on the one hand, and her leadership of the neighborhood watch on the other. Finally, the watch won, and she rolled her eyes. "Oh, all right. If you're going to get all heavy-handed on us."

"So you'll take a closer look at the DLF membership?"

"Yes, of course. Having a murderer in our midst probably is not a good thing."

"I'll say it isn't," said Harriet, as she gave me a curious look.

"What?" I asked, after having endured the look for all of five minutes.

"I thought you were going to call us in when you needed our assistance?"

"I would have," I said. "But it's been one of those days. Hectic, if you see what I mean."

"We've been running around like headless ducks," Dooley added with a knowing nod.

"All right, fine," said Brutus. "Apologies accepted. So what do you want us to do?"

I blinked. It only very rarely happens that Harriet and Brutus put their fate in my paws, and now that it had happened, I was unsure how to proceed. You see, I'm one of those loner cats who like to do things all by themselves. I mean, I have Dooley assisting me, of course, but that's it. I'm not management material. I don't like to boss cats around.

"Well…" I said, thinking hard if there was indeed stuff I could delegate. "Um…"

"Oh, I see," said Harriet, her temper flaring up. "You don't want us around, is that it?"

"No, of course not!" I cried.

"Max wants to have all the glory for himself, tootsie roll," Brutus grunted, giving me a dangerous look. "He wants to be the hero of this investigation—all the credit for himself."

"No, that's not true!" I said. "Okay, look, I was thinking that maybe you can join Gran and Scarlett and infiltrate this duck group. And also, Cotton is holding a press conference this afternoon, and it might be a good idea to spread out and keep tabs on the crowd."

"Way ahead of you, Maxie baby," said Brutus. "And for your information: when the credits are finally awarded, I want it on record that we thought of it first, all right?"

"All right," I said. "Of course."

"So as it stands: we're the ones who are going to nab this vicious killer," said Harriet. "Not you and Dooley. Me and Brutus. Capeesh?"

"Absolutely," I said.

I must say that when the neighborhood watch finally rolled out—or should I say the Duck Liberation Front—I was secretly relieved.

No, I'm definitely not a born leader.

CHAPTER 16

Ebony Pilay lived in a very nice condo on the top floor of a very nice building. It sported a gym, a heated pool, a spa, and even concierge service, whatever that meant. Miss Pilay herself seemed to live alone, and when we walked into her flat it wasn't hard to see why: life-sized pictures of herself adorned the entrance, the main wall of the living room, and even the bedroom. It made me wonder who in their right mind would want to stare at a picture of themselves all the time. And conversely: who in their right mind would date a woman who was so clearly in love with herself?

The supermodel bade our humans to take a seat on a very uncomfortable-looking sofa—built for style, not comfort—and patiently waited until they launched into the interview.

I had to admit she was quite easily as gorgeous in reality as she was in all of those pictures she had used to wallpaper her condo. She had large hazel eyes, the smoothest skin I've ever seen, and silky hair that lay close to her head in the finest curls.

She was dressed in a silver kimono and her feet were slippered in the kind of fluffy bathroom slippers they hand out in fancy hotels. In others words: she had the out-of-bed look down pat, though it wouldn't surprise me if she hadn't been busy getting out of bed for the better part of the morning and had shot an Instagram Story showing her millions of followers how she went about it and had bagged an endorsement deal in the process.

"We talked to Tobias Pushman this morning," said Chase, taking out his little notebook, "and he told us how you made quite a scene in Cotton Karat's office yesterday."

Ebony lifted the corners of her lips fractionally. I think it was her way of smiling. "And can you blame me? The man had just dumped me by text. By text, sergeant!"

"Detective," Chase corrected her gently. "You clearly weren't happy about it."

"Would you be happy if your girlfriend dumped you in such an obscenely rude way?"

"No, I guess I wouldn't," Chase admitted, casting a quick glance to Odelia.

"Look, I can understand that for a man in Cotton's position, a fling doesn't mean a thing, but come on, detective. A little respect, please. Especially when he'd just told me I was the love of his life, and had started murmuring about weddings and honeymoons!"

"Cotton had proposed marriage?"

"Not in so many words," Ebony admitted. "But the man definitely had marriage on his mind when we last spoke." She inclined her head. "Though he did a lot more than speak, if you see what I mean."

"I think I do," said Chase.

"What can I say? The man was enamored with me. Crazy about me. And who wouldn't be? I am a very desirable woman, detective. All men want me, in fact I drive them crazy, and Cotton was no exception. Which is why I was shocked—shocked, I tell you—when he sent me that text. Out of the blue he suddenly broke up with me!"

"And so you stormed into his office and gave him a piece of your mind."

"Yes, I did. But if you're going to conclude from that that I killed him, you're very much mistaken. I would never raise a hand at anyone in anger, detective. I'm a peaceable girl. In fact I abhor violence of any kind." And to prove her words, she rested her hands in her lap and assumed the facial expression of a Buddha. A very beautiful Buddha, of course.

"Can you tell us where you were last night between ten and midnight, Miss Pilay?" asked Odelia.

A small frown appeared on the model's brow, then instantly was gone as she relaxed those all-important facial muscles. "I was here, on the phone with the editors for the next edition of *Vogue*. We were discussing my involvement. It will be my twentieth cover, you see, and we're thinking about doing something really special this time." She waved a delicate hand as she gestured to a framed *Vogue* cover that hung behind Chase and Odelia. "Maybe something with... clouds this time. Or... paint, maybe. Blue paint... or pink."

"We're going to need the name of this editor," said Chase, cutting through this impromptu brainstorming session. "So we can verify your alibi."

"You were on the phone the whole time?" asked Odelia.

"It was a conference call, with several members of the creative team. It didn't run too long, though. A girl needs her beauty sleep. Sleep regenerates collagen, you see." She studied Odelia's face. "I see that you haven't had enough sleep. If you're not careful it will lead to the collagen in your face to break down, which could lead to premature wrinkles."

Odelia inadvertently touched her face, presumably to

keep that collagen from breaking down. "After you left the office yesterday, did you come straight here?"

"No, actually I didn't. I went for a drive."

"Where did you go?"

"Just driving along, you know, with the top down." She smiled. "Now I know what you're thinking, but I did put on sunblock first. In fact I put on sunblock every time I leave the house. And I was wearing sunglasses, of course, to protect my eyes." She carefully touched the tips of her fingers to the puffy part underneath the eyes. She seemed to like what she was feeling, for she smiled again. "You should try sunblock, detective. I don't like the look of those pores. I think your skin might have suffered some damage already."

Chase obviously didn't bother too much about his pores, for he asked, "Can you think of anyone who would want to harm Cotton?"

"Apart from myself, you mean?" she asked finely. "Actually, I do. The man's ex-wife once sent me a very threatening message. I kept it, of course, since a girl in my position has to be extra careful."

She didn't elucidate what her position was, but she did produce her phone, and brought up the message in question.

"Here," she said, placing her phone on the coffee table, which, not coincidentally, also had a very large coffee table book with her face on the cover.

Chase took the phone and read, "'Stay away from my husband. I'm warning you.'"

"There's another one there," said Ebony.

"'If you don't leave my husband alone, I'll rearrange your face and make sure no man will ever look at you again.'"

"The odd thing is that when she wrote that, they were already divorced, so technically Cotton was her ex-husband. But clearly she still feels very proprietary about the man."

"Were you the reason Cotton divorced his wife?" asked

Chase as he took a picture of both messages with his own phone.

"No, of course not. I'm not a homewrecker, detective. When I met Cotton he was already divorced."

"So why did they divorce?" asked Odelia.

Ebony shrugged a pair of shapely shoulders. "You'd have to ask Cotton."

Both Chase and Odelia looked up at this.

"Oh, yes. I know that the man who was killed last night wasn't Cotton but some hapless lookalike," said Ebony as she flicked an imaginary piece of lint from her kimono.

"Who told you?" asked Chase.

"Tobias. He phoned me before you arrived. Turns out it wasn't Cotton's idea to dump me but his so-called advisors. They shipped him off to some rehab clinic and tried to get rid of me—all because some of the Karat shareholders are unhappy with Cotton. All nonsense, if you ask me. Then again, a lot of men are afraid of a woman who wields as much power as I do. Which is exactly what I told Tobias. You see, I know his little secret, and if he and Cotton don't tell the truth at the press conference later today, I'll make sure Tobias's affair with the leader of that duck action front will be front-page news tomorrow." She gracefully rose with a swishing of her kimono. "And now if there's nothing else…"

CHAPTER 17

"I really thought Ebony Pilay would have a cat," said Dooley once we were back in the car, en route to our next destination. "She seems like the type."

"Is there a cat type?" I said. "I wonder."

"Of course," said Dooley. "There's a cat type and a dog type, and Ebony Pilay is definitely the cat type."

"That James Bond villain who was always stroking his cat, was he the cat type?" I mused. "Ernst Stavro Blofeld. Always trying to dominate the world by launching rockets at some far-flung destination."

Dooley gave me a curious look. "Do you think Ebony Pilay is actually a James Bond villain in disguise?"

"I shouldn't wonder," I said. "She struck me as a very villainy type, to be honest."

"So... do you think all cat types are villains in disguise?"

We looked at Odelia. Of course, since we were in the backseat, all we could see was the back of her head, but it suddenly struck me as very villainy indeed. But then she turned and gave us both a dazzling smile, tickled us under our chins, and turned to face the front again.

Dooley and I shared a look of intense relief. "Definitely not a villain," I said.

"Definitely."

"So maybe Odelia is the exception that proves the rule."

"You mean she's the only cat person in the world who isn't a villain?"

"It's possible," I said. It was a revolutionary thought, of course. Until now I'd always thought that dog people were all villains, but now I was starting to think the opposite was true. And it stood to reason: dogs are notoriously dumb creatures, whereas cats are clever and, dare I say, even devious, to a certain extent.

Clever, devious, gorgeous, fastidious... all traits of a supervillain.

In other words: if Odelia hadn't taken me in, I might have been Blofeld's pet!

It boggled the mind to even contemplate such a horrendous contingency.

We had finally arrived at destination's end, and after taking a few wrong turns, with Chase freely cursing the GPS and Odelia coming to his assistance by using an app on her phone, the Heartfield Clinic loomed up large before us.

"This place once belonged to a local sausage king," said Odelia, reading from her phone. "But after a dozen people died from eating his sausages he went bust and sold the place to a philanthropist who launched the Heartfield Clinic."

"Do they only treat sex addicts here?" asked Chase as he parked his car between a Rolls Royce and a Jaguar.

"No, all kinds of addicts," said Odelia. "They're not choosy."

"I wonder if they also treat meat addiction," said Dooley

as we hopped from the backseat and gracefully landed on the cobbled ground.

"Meat isn't an addiction, Dooley," I said. "Cats need meat. We're carnivores, after all."

"But Gran said that meat is very bad. In fact she says that meat is murder."

"Gran has some strange ideas sometimes," I said. "Though it probably is true that people in general eat too much meat. There are other foods they could eat but don't."

"Maybe we should become vegetarians, too," said Dooley. "I mean, poor ducks."

"Yeah, poor ducks," I said, thinking back to that nice Fred the duck, pining in his stall back at the duck farm. "At the very least they could allow them to roam free."

"Maybe Gran and Scarlett should stage a breakout? Free the ducks?"

"Please don't mention that to them. They might just go ahead and do it."

We'd entered the clinic, which was airy and bright and clean inside, with a woman dressed like a nurse behind the reception, who greeted us with a radiant smile.

"What can I do for you?" she said, and I could see she was already sizing us up: were we addicted to sex, drugs, alcohol or some other more exotic substance? Glue, perhaps?

The moment Chase produced his badge, and so did Odelia, the woman's smile diminished somewhat. "Oh," she said. Addicted to law and order. Probably incurable.

"We're here to see Cotton Karat," said Chase. "We believe he's expecting us."

"Of course," said the woman, much sobered. Like most people, she didn't enjoy coming face to face with the long arm of the law, or even the strong arm of the law. "Please take a seat."

And so we took a seat.

"I wonder if Uncle Alec shouldn't give us badges, too," said Dooley. "It would make life a lot easier for us."

"We don't need badges, Dooley," I said. "We're cats, and cats can sneak into any place, no questions asked. It's the humans they're adamant to keep out for some reason."

We glanced around, then Dooley said, "I think it's more that they want to keep people in." And he was right, of course. Clinics like Heartfield want to keep those addicts in, and prevent them from wreaking havoc on an unsuspecting society. Though as far as I understood, Cotton Karat didn't actually suffer any addiction. The sex addiction thing was just a pretext to remove him from circulation for the time being, while the shareholders all calmed down and stopped the stock price from dropping like the proverbial stone.

It took about ten minutes for the staff to track down Cotton, but then we were led outside into the garden, and moments later we were seated on a nice bench next to the fallen business tycoon, looking out across a field of green as far as the eye could see.

"Nice place," said Chase.

"Oh, absolutely," said Cotton. "You'd almost think you're on vacation here, if it wasn't for the people screaming the house down in the middle of the night and having to be restrained." He sighed. "Tobias told me they're getting me out of here—and not a moment too soon, I can tell you."

"So I take it you heard about what happened with Eric Blandine?"

"Yeah, poor schmuck. What are the chances, right?"

"So you think they were gunning for you?"

"Of course. Blandine was just a lowly worker drone as far as I can tell. Who would want to kill him? Whereas I am in charge of a multimillion-dollar company. Of course I was the intended target. I hope Tobias has learned his lesson and is going to tighten my security. If you think I'm looking forward to having my liver removed you're very much mistaken." He glowered at no one in particular, arms folded across his chest.

He was a handsome man, this Cotton Karat. Wavy dark hair, refined features, patrician nose, eyes that some people would have described as molten chocolate when they were smoldering as they were now. And of course an athletic body, as evidenced by rolling biceps stretching the pink polo shirt he was wearing.

"Do you have any idea who could have done this to… Blandine?" said Odelia. She'd almost said 'to you' but of course nothing had been done to Cotton. It was the 'lowly worker drone' who'd gotten it in the neck, poor guy. No stock options for him.

"Take your pick," said Cotton, gesticulating angrily. "Upset shareholders, those crazy duck lovers, angry investors…"

"Your ex-wife Dawn?" Odelia suggested.

Cotton looked up at this. "Dawn? What makes you think that?"

"We talked to Ebony Pilay just now," said Chase. "And she said she's received several threatening messages sent by Dawn. Threats that might extend to you, since you're the one who divorced her."

Cotton smoothed his shirt. "She wasn't happy with me, that's for sure. But murder? I don't know, detective. That seems a little excessive, even for Dawn."

"Why did you divorce her?"

"Because we were through. Simply speaking, I fell out of love with Dawn. Well, you know how it is. When you meet a person for the first time, you're madly in love, and you think she's the only girl in the world. But then you get to know her, and the love light gradually fades, until one day you wake up next to a complete stranger, and wonder what you saw in her in the first place. And also, Dawn really let herself go after we had Inari."

"Your daughter."

Cotton nodded. "You should have seen her when we met. She was gorgeous. But then she got fat and ugly, and even though I told her on several occasions to get her act together..."

"You told her she was fat and ugly?" asked Odelia incredulously.

"I believe in the power of truth, Mrs. Kingsley," said the CEO, unrepentant. "If you can't handle the truth, you have no business being alive. And Dawn, I'm afraid to say, didn't take it well." He lowered the collar of his shirt and showed us a tiny scar. "Threw a mirror at me." He shrugged. "So I gave her an ultimatum. Drop thirty pounds or I'd divorce her. She told me to go and boil my head, so we got divorced."

"I don't think I like Cotton Karat very much, Max," said Dooley.

"No, me neither," I said, giving the man a dark look.

"So how about Ebony Pilay?" asked Chase, since Odelia seemed too mad to continue asking questions.

"What about her?"

"She was pretty angry with you."

"Not with me. With my entourage."

"She didn't know it wasn't you who dumped her."

"I guess not," he said with a frown. "Do you think she killed that sap Blandine?"

"Do you?"

"Mh. She's got a temper, Ebony has, but murder? I don't know... She's crazy about me, you know. As am I about her."

"Do you think you'll get back together?"

Cotton slapped his thighs and heaved a deep sigh. "I wish. My dad has really tightened the screws. If I ever go near Ebony again he's going to kick me out of the company, and

I'm afraid he's not kidding this time. I mean…" He gestured around. "He practically kidnapped me and put me in this institution! That must be some kind of human rights violation." He gave Chase a hopeful look. "Should I press charges? Surely people have gone to jail for less?"

But Chase wasn't allowing himself to be drawn into this family dispute. "Ebony seems to think you'll be an item again."

"Well, she can think again. I'm not going anywhere near that woman. I mean, I don't want to lose everything over a piece of skirt."

Suddenly Odelia got up and stomped off. We all watched her leave, and it could have been my imagination but I had the distinct impression smoke was coming from her ears.

"You're a real piece of work, aren't you, Mr. Karat?" said Chase, shaking his head.

"I'm just saying it like it is, detective. You're thinking it, and I'm saying it."

"Oh, no," said Chase. "This is all you, Cotton."

"Fine. So I'm the last honest man on the planet. Sue me. Are we done?"

"Yeah," said Chase, getting up and glowering at the man. "We're done."

CHAPTER 18

"What a nasty piece of work!" Odelia fumed once we were en route to Hampton Cove again. "I can't believe what Ebony sees in the guy!"

"He's rich, handsome, and I'm sure he can be charming when he wants to be," said Chase.

"Well, he's not fooling me. And in my next article I'm going to lay it all out, no holds barred."

Chase chuckled. "Looks like Cotton is in for some more trouble."

"He's got it coming. What a thoroughly despicable person."

"I think it's all that foie gras he eats," said Dooley. "Eating that much liver can't be healthy. It probably affects his own liver and now he's turned into a grinch."

"Not a grinch," I corrected my friend. "More like a misogynist."

"That sounds bad," said Dooley, eyeing me curiously. "Is that like cancer?"

"Absolutely," I said with a smile. "A cancer to society."

"So where are we going now?" I asked, addressing my

question to Odelia since Chase still didn't speak our language for some reason, even though he'd been rubbing shoulders with us for a while now.

"We're going to talk to the rest of the family," said Odelia. "Cotton's dad, ex-wife and daughter. Find out what they have to say about this murder business."

"I hope Harriet and Brutus are all right," said Dooley. "Infiltrating a duck group could be dangerous, especially if one of them is a killer."

"I'm sure they'll be fine," I said, though I did experience a slight twinge of unease, too. Going undercover in a group of animal rights activists did indeed sound like a mission fraught with danger. I just hoped that these duck rights activists would extend their love of ducks to other species of animals, too. Like cats. Then again, bird lovers are often the most virulent cat haters, since they seem to think we alone are to blame for the decimation of the bird population. Even though personally I don't know any cats who'd want to be seen dead with a duck, so hopefully that gave these duck people pause when they went on their rampage.

Diedrich Karat lived in a house easily as big and nice as the entire Heartfield Clinic. His wife, Cotton's mom, had died some years ago, so the businessman had the house all to himself.

"He must have sold a lot of foie gras to afford a place like this," said Dooley when we were staring up at the facade, which consisted of dark brick which lent it a touch of ominousness. Like those dark and stormy night stories the Brontë sisters liked so much. When the door opened I half expected a tortured-looking Heathcliff to be staring back at us, eyes burning like lumps of coal. Instead, it was just a regular butler with no visible signs of insanity.

"It's not just foie gras the Karats are selling," I said as we followed our humans across the threshold and into the Karat dwelling. "They're a luxury goods company, which means they sell everything your rich person likes, be it expensive watches, cars, jewelry, clothes, shoes, perfume, tobacco products… If it's expensive and exclusive, the Karats will sell it."

"Are there so many rich people in the world who can afford that kind of stuff?"

"Oh, absolutely. There are plenty of billionaires and even more millionaires."

"Is Odelia a millionaire?"

"No, not exactly," I said with a smile. "Not on a reporter's salary."

"If she works hard enough, and saves enough money, do you think she'll ever be a millionaire?"

"It's possible," I said. "But only if she lives to be five hundred years old."

Dooley thought about this for a moment. "I don't think humans live that long, do they?"

"No, they don't."

"Pity."

Diedrich was waiting for us in what the butler called the smoking room. Fortunately for us no smoking was going on at that moment, since smoking irritates my sensitive sense of smell.

Cotton's dad was one of those barrel-chested men. He was also one of those potbellied men, and the combination of that barrel chest and that potbelly made him look very big indeed. In contrast, he had a rather small head and spindly legs, and so the end result was disconcerting.

He got up from a squeaky leather couch with some effort, and greeted us with a kindly smile and an outstretched hand. "How did you find Cotton? In good spirits, I hope?"

"He seemed fine," said Odelia, perhaps a little more curtly than a loving father might have hoped.

Diedrich must have picked up on it, for he said, "He hates it there, I know. But it is for his own good. You can't go around frolicking all over the stage in front of a room full of shareholders and expect them to like it. Cotton singlehandedly collapsed our stock. So we had to do something."

"He's giving a press conference this afternoon?" asked Chase.

"Yes, after what happened with Eric Blandine we owe it to our investors to talk turkey. It's very unfortunate but it can't be helped."

"Will you come out of retirement, sir?" asked Odelia.

"I don't think so. My health isn't what I would like it to be. High blood pressure. The doctors have advised me to take a backseat. Let others take the reins from now on."

"So Cotton again?"

"Yes, Cotton again. Only this time we'll keep him on a much tighter leash. No more canoodling with young models in front of the world's cameras. He has a lot of growing up to do, but I'm confident we'll get him there yet." He gave Chase and Odelia an expectant look. "So? What have you found so far? Any imminent arrests I should know about?"

"Not yet, sir," said Chase.

Diedrich frowned. "I thought you were here to give me an update?"

"We're here as part of the investigation. Collect background information on your son and the people that are closest to him—like you, sir, and his ex-wife and daughter."

"What good is that going to do? You should be out there, hunting the bastard down!"

The man's head had turned red, and I could see a vein throbbing in his neck.

"If he keeps this up he'll drop dead before the interview is over," said Dooley.

"Both Chase and Odelia know CPR," I said. "They'll give him the kiss of life."

"What's the kiss of life?" asked Dooley, much interested.

"Mouth-to-mouth resuscitation." When he continued mystified, I explained, "When a person collapses you put your mouth on theirs and breathe into their lungs. In the meantime you give them a heart massage to keep the old ticker going until the paramedics arrive. It's saved a lot of lives."

Dooley studied the Karat patriarch's lips, and shivered. "That can't be hygienic," he said.

"Why not? Odelia kisses Chase all the time."

"Yes, but that's because she makes allowances: because she loves him. But I don't think they love Diedrich, do they?"

"It's not about love, Dooley. It's about saving a life."

"But cooties, Max! Think about the cooties!"

Luckily Chase managed to calm the man down, and his face lost its dark color.

"It's just a routine part of our inquiry, sir," said the cop. "Now can you tell us if your son has any enemies that you know of? Apart from those angry shareholders, of course."

"Well, Ebony Pilay was pretty upset with him, at least according to Tobias. And then there's those duck people. The Duck Liberation Army or whatever they're called."

"Duck Liberation Front," Odelia corrected him.

"It must be them, right? They're the ones who sent Blandine's liver to the office."

"The person in charge of the Duck Liberation Front has a solid alibi," said Chase. "So it can't have been her."

"So one of her followers did it. They're all nuts, as far as I'm concerned. Absolutely bonkers. Who would want to save a duck? You might as well try and save the pigeons. Though

I'm sure there's probably a Pigeon Liberation Front out there as well. Or even a Rat Liberation Army. The world has gone stark-raving mad, that's all I can think."

Dooley turned to me with a questioning look on his face, but even before he could speak, I said, "No, there is no Pigeon Liberation Front or Rat Liberation Army, Dooley. At least I don't think there is."

"There should be, though, wouldn't you agree? Those poor pigeons having to beg for corn kernels and those poor rats having to sniff around dumpsters and stuff."

I sighed. "I'm sure both pigeons and rats are perfectly happy with their lot in life."

"Are you planning to increase security now that Cotton is returning home?" asked Chase.

"Oh, absolutely. Tobias is handling all of that. And I hope he doesn't screw up," the retired business mogul added in a threatening tone. "Or else I'll have his hide."

Dooley chuckled quietly. "They'll have to start a Tobias Liberation Front soon," he said.

CHAPTER 19

Even though Cotton had pretty much dumped his wife like one does a pair of old socks, Dawn Karat hadn't suffered financially in the divorce, as the big pile where she lived proved. It wasn't as grand as Pop Karat's place, but it was nothing to be sniffed at either.

The former Mrs. Cotton Karat received us in what she called her library, though I didn't see a lot of books in evidence. Instead the shelves were loaded with DVDs.

I saw that Dawn still hadn't lost those thirty pounds, and probably had gained another thirty since the divorce, but she was still a handsome woman. She was dressed in a colorful flowing kaftan and was wearing a silk scarf around her head. Shiny gold earrings peeped from beneath the scarf, and she looked as healthy as she did happy.

In fact it wasn't too much to say the woman was absolutely radiant.

"So they cut out his liver and shipped it off to his own office, did they?" she asked. "How ghastly!" But her beaming smile belied her words. "How absolutely ghoulish."

"Where were you last night between ten and midnight,

Mrs. Karat?" asked Chase. But if he'd hoped to put a dent in the woman's sheer delight, he was disappointed.

"I was right here, of course. A real homebody, me."

"Can anyone vouch for you?"

"My daughter, and a brace of servants. In fact Inari and I watched one of our favorite movies last night. *Bedazzled!* You know, about the man who sells his soul to the devil." She winked. "Remind you of someone?"

"If you're referring to your ex-husband…"

"Of course! Though in his case he couldn't sell his soul since he never had one to begin with. Or a heart, for that matter. Oh, there you are, sweetie. These people are from the police. They've come to question us about that gruesome murder."

A young woman had entered the room, looking a lot like her mother. Though she wasn't dressed in a kaftan but simple ripped jeans and a sweater. Her hair hung loose around her shoulders and she wore no makeup to speak of. She was pretty enough to pull it off. Not supermodel pretty, but beautiful in a wholesome way. She took a seat next to her mom, toed off her sneakers and sat cross-legged. "So was it really Dad they tried to kill?"

"Absolutely!" said her mother. "The man who died was pretending to be your dad, wasn't he?"

"Will he be all right?" asked the young woman. "Dad, I mean. Is he being protected?"

"He's fine," Dawn assured her. "They're not going to let another madman near him now, are they?" There was a touch of wistfulness in her voice. "The policeman just asked me where I was last night."

"Here," said Inari immediately. "We were watching *Bedazzled.*"

"Inari is studying to be a film director," Dawn explained.

"So we've been watching a lot of movies together, haven't we, darling?"

Inari nodded, and chewed a thoughtful fingernail. "So was it the duck people who killed that man? Did you arrest them?"

"The investigation is ongoing," said Chase. "Right now we're trying to paint a picture of your father's life."

Dawn laughed at this, going so far as to throw her head back. "Just round up a couple of dozen models and there you have Cotton's life!" she cried. "In that sense Cotton is exactly like Hugh Hefner. Only Hugh had the decency to stay loyal to whoever he was married to at the time, which is more than can be said about Cotton."

"Mom, please," said Inari, looking embarrassed at her mother's outburst.

"It's true, isn't it? The man is in a clinic for sex addicts, darling. That tells you all you need to know about him."

"Yeah, but he's not actually being treated for a sex addiction, is he? That's just a ruse to get him out of the way for a while. Until all this hubbub dies down."

"Is it true that they told the Pilay woman to pack her bags and buzz off?" asked Dawn.

"Not in those terms," said Chase reluctantly.

"Well, good riddance. Parasites, every last one of them. All trying to bleed him dry."

"He never should have left us," said Inari. "If he'd stayed here he wouldn't be in this mess."

"Your father could never resist a pretty face," said Dawn as she studied her own nails. She frowned when she caught her daughter nibbling a cuticle and slapped her hand away. "Bad habit," she muttered. "Her exams are coming up," she said apologetically. "She always gets nervous. For no reason, because she's a brilliant student."

"It's only midterms," Inari murmured.

"So Ebony Pilay told us that you sent her some threatening messages," said Odelia, trying to get the interview back on track.

"Oh, that," said Dawn with a throwaway gesture that made her gold bangles jangle. "I was just trying to make sure she didn't expect too much from Cotton's latest infatuation."

"You've been divorced how long now?" asked Chase.

Dawn pursed her lips. "Four years."

"'Stay away from my husband,'" Chase read from his phone. He looked up at the woman. "You've been divorced four years and you still send threatening messages to your ex-husband's girlfriends?"

"You carry a torch for a person, detective, and even though that person no longer wants to stay married, you don't simply turn off that affection."

"You still love Cotton?"

"Let's just say I care deeply for him. And I don't like it when people take advantage."

"So you thought Miss Pilay was taking advantage of him?"

"Of course. They all do. If Cotton wasn't a Karat, do you really think these girls would be all over him? They're after his money, and his standing in society. All of them imagine themselves becoming the next Mrs. Cotton Karat. Well, there is only one Mrs. Cotton Karat and that's me." She'd tilted her chin and was throwing down the gauntlet, as if daring anyone to contradict her. As it was, both Odelia and Chase kept schtum, letting the silence drag on. Finally Dawn said, "Okay, so I'm a caring person. In fact I probably care too much, and much too deeply. But what can I do? That's the way I'm built. Isn't that right, petal?"

"Oh, Mom," said Inari, and gave her mother a stroke on the arm.

"And what about you, Miss Karat?" asked Odelia. "Do you still care about your dad?"

"What kind of a question is that!" Dawn burst out, but Inari smiled.

"Of course I do. He's my dad, isn't he? And frankly I don't care about the girlfriends or the glitzy parties or the fancy cars he likes to drive. When it's just the two of us that all falls away. He's just my dad, you know, and I know he loves me and I love him."

"He's not a bad person," said Dawn. "He's just... immature, I guess. And I blame Deirdre and Diedrich. They spoiled him and they spoiled Jared. Spoiled them both rotten."

"Uncle Jared is different, though," said Inari. "He's got an artist's soul."

Dawn scoffed at this, but when her daughter gave her a critical look, she masked it by coughing into her fist. "He's different, all right," she said. "And also the same, of course."

CHAPTER 20

That afternoon, emotions were running high in anticipation of the press conference Cotton was holding after the murder of the man who was hired to replace him. Rumors and innuendo were flying around the room of the press center, and reporters were clamoring for a good seat so they could launch a barrage of questions at the beleaguered business tycoon.

When Cotton finally walked on stage, half an hour late, he looked fine, and so did Tobias Pushman, who took a seat next to his CEO. Diedrich didn't put in an appearance, though I saw him hover at the edge of the stage. He didn't look so hot, but then high-pressure situations were probably a big no-no for the man's high blood pressure.

And then, much to everyone's surprise, Inari Karat also joined her dad on stage.

"She didn't mention she was going to participate," Odelia told Chase.

"She probably didn't think it was important," Chase reciprocated.

There's often a vast chasm between what witnesses think

is important and what the police deem so. And more often than not it concerns things those witnesses prefer to keep a secret for whatever reason.

Since Odelia and Chase were in the first row, so were Dooley and I, which afforded us an excellent vantage point to follow this all-important briefing.

"As you are probably aware," said Cotton, addressing the room full of journos, "a man was murdered late last night. This man was an employee of the Karat Group. His name is Eric Blandine and he was a much-appreciated and hard-working member of the Karat family. Let's please observe a minute of silence in remembrance of Mr. Blandine." He inclined his head and folded his hands in prayer. All of five seconds later, he looked up again. "Eric Blandine put his life on the line for this company, and I think we can all appreciate his family's bereavement, so I'm going to ask you to respect their privacy."

"I thought Cotton thought that Eric Blandine was just a lowly worker drone?" asked Dooley.

"I have the impression Eric Blandine is about to become canonized," I said.

"Mr. Blandine stepped forward at a time when the Karat family found itself under duress. My relationship with Ebony Pilay recently broke down, and I found myself unable to cope with this personal tragedy that had befallen me. So I decided that I needed some time to come to terms with the loss and take a break. But of course the Karat Group needs leadership. And so Eric volunteered to provide this leadership at this difficult time. In so doing he provided the group with an essential service, and me with much-needed time to grieve. I will answer questions later," he snapped when three hands rose up in the room.

"He's lying through his teeth," said Dooley.

"He's being creative with the truth," I said. "It's called PR."

"So PR is like creative lying?"

"Something like that."

"And of course we know what happened next. Some dastardly criminals decided to take Eric's life last night, a life he sacrificed for the group he worked his entire life for. The company he served with honor and dignity. With pride and dedication. Let's take another minute to commemorate such a remarkable man." Three seconds later, he went on, "Because of what happened, I've decided to cut my break short, and assume full control of the group once more. There is a time to grieve, but there's also a time to take one's responsibility. The Karat Group employs fifty thousand people across the globe. They deserve a strong leader. A leader who will make sure that the people who took Eric Sardine away from us will be punished to the fullest extent of the law. It's what Eric Sardine deserves. It's what Eric Sardine died for." He bowed his head nobly.

"It's Blandine!" we could hear Tobias hiss, even though he held his hand over his mic.

Cotton looked up again, his mournful expression replaced by a smile. "And now my daughter would like to say a few words. Inari?"

And as the youngest scion of the Karat family took the stage, the reporter to Odelia's right leaned over and whispered, "This holier-than-thou attitude is making me sick!"

"Whose? Cotton's?"

"The daughter, of course."

"Why?"

"She pretends to be all lovey-dovey with the world, but I saw her go toe-to-toe with the girlfriend only last week. Shouting abuse at her like some truck driver. Who would have thought that a girl who looks like a saint would know language as foul as that!"

"Are you sure it was Inari?" asked Odelia, clearly surprised.

"Absolutely. Told the Pilay woman that she was a right so-and-so and that if she didn't stay away from her dad she would cut off her head and stick it up her you-know-what!"

We all stared at Inari, who was smiling sweetly, and telling the congregation how important her father's values had always been to her and that he was a shining example of the true business leader. She also hinted she was considering a change of career so the next generation of Karats would be ready to take the group into the future and beyond.

"I thought she wanted to be the next Steven Spielberg?" said Dooley.

"Looks like she wants to be the next Cotton Karat instead," I said.

"Let's all give a warm round of applause to my father—the incomparable Cotton Karat!" Inari finished her speech.

There was lukewarm applause from a few of the journalists—the ones writing for the women's magazines, most notably—but then hands rose up and the shouting started as a barrage of questions were shot, like bullets, at the collected Karats on stage.

"Tough crowd," I said as a reporter asked if it was true that Ebony Pilay had been dumped by text and another asked if it was true that Eric Blandine had been a forklift driver in one of the Karat warehouses until a couple of days ago, and had been called Goldie by his colleagues on account of his remarkable likeness with Cotton himself.

You can try to PR yourself out of a mess, but sooner or later the truth will out.

The press conference finally over, Odelia and Chase hurried to the side of the stage, hoping to have a quick word with Cotton. But when we arrived there, the man was being chewed out by his dad.

"An unmitigated disaster!" Diedrich was hissing, spittle flying into Cotton's face. "You couldn't even remember the guy's name, for Christ's sakes!"

"Blandine, Sardine—who cares?"

"They care!" Diedrich said, pointing in the direction of the room. "I can imagine what they'll be writing about this train wreck. Your second train-wreck performance in the space of a week! If you keep this up the stock price will hit rock bottom by this time tomorrow! And what were you thinking to drag Inari up on stage with you!"

"It's called future-proofing the business, Dad."

"She doesn't have the skills! And besides, she doesn't want to take over the business."

"She'll do what I tell her to do," said Cotton stubbornly.

"You are such a moron," his dad grumbled.

Chase and Odelia decided that under the circumstances perhaps it was better to postpone their questions to a later date. At least if Diedrich hadn't murdered his son by then.

CHAPTER 21

It had been a long day full of interviews and not a lot of toilet breaks or naps, so when the time to head out to cat choir rolled around, I found myself hesitating. A nice long nap on the couch sounded very appealing. Then again, having a little chat with my fellow cats is one of those pleasures of life it's hard to say no to.

So as the moon rose in the sky, to paint the tops of the trees a milky white, Dooley and I made our way to the playground which is located in the heart of the park, and soon were relaxing atop the jungle gym.

Shanille, cat choir's conductor, was frowning as she tried to decide on the musical program for the night, and our friends were all chattering excitedly, as only cats can, blithely ignoring those few neighbors who like to try and spoil the fun by throwing some old shoes in our direction. They don't seem to realize that cats don't even wear shoes!

"I'm very disappointed in you, Max," said Harriet as she gave me her best frowny face.

"Oh? And why is that?" I said, trying to balance on top of that jungle gym. It was harder than I thought. Usually I prefer to stay safely on the ground. For a cat as big-boned as me having to position his body on a narrow metal tube is always a challenge.

"I'm bored, that's why! No suspects to talk to, no clues to suss out. I feel so useless!"

"Me, too," said Brutus, giving me a dark look. "I'm a cop cat, Max. I'm the one who should be out there with Chase, hunting down this liver-eating maniac."

"He didn't actually eat the liver," said Dooley. "He just put it in a tin."

"All the same, it's me who should tag along with the police squad, not you guys."

"What can I say?" I said. "Odelia likes to have us around. And four cats is too much."

"Says who?" Harriet demanded heatedly.

"Says anyone. Imagine a cop with four cats on their trail. It's like the punchline of a joke."

"Tom Hanks had Hooch," said Brutus. "And Hooch was as big as a dozen cats."

"Hooch was a dog, and people are used to seeing cops with dogs," I argued.

"Max is right," said Dooley. "People always give Odelia a strange look when she walks in with her two cats."

"Okay, fine," said Harriet. "But at least we should have a chance to participate. Why not flip a coin? Then one day you can join Odelia, and the next it's me and Brutus."

"Yeah, it's only fair that we get to tag along for a change," Brutus grumbled. "Now you and Dooley are hogging all the attention. It's just not fair."

"But what about your undercover mission? I thought you were looking forward to infiltrating the Duck Liberation Front?"

"Nothing doing. As long as Eric Blandine's killer hasn't been caught, Lita Fiol has suspended all DLF activities. She says she doesn't want to have another murder on her conscience."

"So she thinks it's one of her members?" I asked.

"Looks like," said Harriet. "Though a fat lot of good that'll do us. There's no way we'll be able to find out who it is."

"Lita was ordered to hand over a list of members," I said. "So chances are the killer is among them."

"So?"

"So you can go and visit them one by one and spy on them." When both Harriet and Brutus gave me an unhappy grimace, I said, "It's bona fide detective work. In fact it's probably more important than what we've been doing all day."

"It was moderately boring," said Dooley. "Odelia and Chase talked to people, and then they talked to some more people, and then some more. In fact all they did all day was talk. And still we didn't get anywhere."

"That's also part of being a detective," I said. "Try to find out who was where, when and why. It's boring but essential. As is studying police reports, poring over forensic evidence, and trying to find a connection to all the elements pertaining to the case."

"And here I thought being a detective was all about finding the missing clue," Brutus grumbled. "A nice footprint, a fingerprint, or a little-known toxin in the victim's blood."

"See!" Dooley cried. "I knew it! He was poisoned!"

"No, he wasn't," I said. "He was stabbed to death."

"Oh," said Dooley, slumping a little. He cut a glance to Harriet. "Boring, Harriet."

"I hear you, Dooley," said our Persian friend, but she suddenly looked a lot less harried.

Dooley was right, though. Police work can be boring, and most of it feels like looking for a needle in a haystack. But it's important to put in the work, even though sometimes it feels useless. But as long as you take enough naps, and there's always plenty of kibble to keep you going, it's fine by me. I like to discover those human foibles that make them tick, or to listen to them gossip about other people. Or being caught out in a blatant lie.

It's all very human, isn't it? But then murder is a very human thing.

Kingman came clambering up the jungle gym, then thought better of it and decided to remain on terra firma. Kingman is a big cat, and even though in the actual jungle big cats like to climb trees and take a nap there, in Hampton Cove big cats stick to the ground.

So instead I climbed down and left Harriet, Brutus and Dooley to exchange plaintive stories about how boring it is to be a pet detective.

"Hey, buddy," I said once I'd joined my friend. "How are things at the General Store?"

"Not so good," said Kingman. "Wilbur caught another pickpocket today. It's the third one in a week. And the more he catches, the more seem to crawl out of the woodwork."

"A pickpocket? Not a thief?"

"No, an actual pickpocket. They position themselves behind a customer who's squeezing an orange or reading the fine print on a packet of chips, stick their hands in their pockets and come away with their wallets. Or their phones or whatever. According to the cop who came over to make the arrest, it's a regular plague. They're all over town."

"Probably some gang," I said. "They seem to travel in packs, these pickpockets."

"Yeah, but it's frustrating. People seem to think it's Wilbur's fault."

"I very much doubt that, Kingman."

"No, but they do. They figure that if they're being robbed, it's because Wilbur didn't do enough to keep these people out. But there's only so much you can do. You can't look at a person's face and know they're going to try and rob your customers, can you?"

"No, I guess not," I said. His words seem to ring a bell in my head, for some reason, though for the life of me I couldn't quite grasp it.

I decided to drop it for now.

It would come to me.

Or not.

CHAPTER 22

The next morning, we decided to pay another visit to Diedrich Karat, since we had the impression the man had been less than honest with us the first time around.

"Why is it that people lie all the time, Max?" asked Dooley as we entered the man's lair.

"Because they're afraid that if the police find out the truth, it will make them look guilty," I said. "Or maybe they have some skeletons hidden in their closet they don't want anyone to know about."

"Skeletons in their closets?" asked Dooley, his eyes swiveling to a nearby cupboard. He took a step back, as if expecting the cupboard to open and the skeleton to tumble out.

"Okay, so Cotton wasn't exactly my first pick as my successor," the old man admitted. "But what could I do? There's always been a Karat at the helm of the Karat Group."

"Why doesn't Cotton's brother Jared step up?" asked Chase.

"Jared is a numbers man. He's not interested in taking the

lead. And besides, he doesn't have the chops. It's not so easy to lead a company of these dimensions."

"What's going to happen now?" asked Odelia.

Diedrich shrugged. He looked as if he'd shrunk a little overnight. His cheeks were hollow and so were his eyes. He'd probably been up half the night thinking about the future of his company. "Maybe Tobias is right. Maybe we should get an outsider to run the company. A proven leader. Cotton is clearly not up to the task, and neither is Jared."

"What about Inari? Cotton seems to want her to take over."

"Out of the question. Inari's interests lie elsewhere."

Just then, Inari walked in. When she saw us, she halted. "Oh, I didn't know you had company, Grandpa."

"It's all right, sweetheart. It's the police."

"Yeah, I know," said Inari, giving us a curious look.

"We were surprised to find that you're interested in taking over the business," said Odelia. "You didn't mention that when we talked to you and your mother yesterday."

"Yeah, my dad asked me to say a few words at his big press conference, so we decided to tell them what he thought they wanted to hear."

"In other words, your dad asked you to lie for him?"

She darted a quick look to her grandfather, but when he nodded she relented. "It's not really lying. I might take an interest in the company at some point. After all, the movie industry and the luxury goods industry have a lot in common. So our futures might converge at some point."

"Rubbish," said Diedrich. "Don't listen to your dad with his twisted ideas of the truth, honey. You just do what you want to do, and let us figure out how to get out of this mess."

"Are you sure? Because Dad seems to feel I have a lot to contribute."

"Yes, I'm sure. Your dad has wasted his life in the pursuit

of idle passions. Please don't make the same mistake. You just follow your heart, sweetheart. And forget about this convergence nonsense."

Inari seemed to perk up at this. She took a seat on the couch next to her granddad, only when she put her sneakers up onto that fine leather, he gave her a not-so-grandfatherly look and she quickly lowered them to the floor again.

"There's one more thing we need to ask you, Inari," said Odelia. "Is it true that you and Ebony Pilay were engaged in an argument last week? You were heard telling her to stay away from your dad or else."

"You used some very strong language, according to a witness we spoke to," said Chase.

The girl had the decency to blush. "I may have said a few things in the heat of the moment," she said. "But she had it coming," she rallied. "All she's interested in is my dad's money. If he wasn't *the* Cotton Karat she wouldn't give him the time of day."

"The same thing can be said for most of the women my son has dated," Diedrich pointed out.

"Ebony Pilay is a horrible person," said Inari, "as everyone who knows her will tell you. I happen to know her ex-PA, and he said she's the worst person in the world. She made him work day and night, paid him a pittance, and treated him like dirt."

"Look, if your dad wants to date women like that, it's his funeral," said Diedrich.

This made Odelia and Chase raise their eyebrows in surprise. "Wasn't it your idea to break off the affair by sending your son into rehab, sir?" asked Chase.

Diedrich grunted, "Tobias came up with that one. But sometimes you have to admit a person is beyond salvage. Cotton isn't six years old anymore. I can't make him behave."

"What are you going to do, Grandpa?" asked Inari, affectionately placing her head on her grandfather's shoulder.

"I don't know, child. But it looks as if we're going to have to cut your dad loose."

"What do you mean?"

"Remove him from the company once and for all. In other words: sever all ties. Professionally, at least," he added for Odelia and Chase's sake. "Cotton will always be a beloved son, but maybe not the Karat Group CEO anymore. After all, enough is enough."

CHAPTER 23

We met up with Jared Karat at the office. The man might not have an office as nice as his brother Cotton, but it was still nice and big enough. Jared was the company's CFO, which meant that he was in charge of the group's financial affairs.

"Shoot," said Jared once we were all settled in. He'd raised his eyebrows when Odelia and Chase had waltzed in, accompanied by two cats, but then a man who works for a luxury goods company probably doesn't bat an eye at the peculiarities of his customers.

He looked a lot like his brother, actually, only his face was more lined, and the horn-rimmed round glasses he wore lent him a more intellectual aspect. He was dressed to impress, though, in a Brooks Brothers suit if I wasn't mistaken.

"Your dad tells us that you have no interest in being CEO," said Chase, not beating about the bush. "Why is that, exactly?"

The man smiled. "Is this the part where you're going to get all Freudian on me and tell me I harbor a deep-seated grudge against my older brother and have wanted to smother him since I was in the cradle?"

Chase gave him an indulgent smile in return. "I'm just curious to know why a man as obviously successful and intelligent as yourself wouldn't be more ambitious."

"I see. Now you're asking me why my dad allows a loose cannon like Cotton to run the company into the ground while he's got a perfectly balanced member of his offspring waiting in the wings, jumping at the chance to take over."

"That's not what I said."

Jared took off his glasses and carefully polished them. I saw he had the same chocolate eyes as his brother. "Look, I have absolutely no desire to run this company. I'm a numbers guy—always have been. I love to stay on top of everything and make sure things run smoothly. But I have no interest in flying across the world visiting factories, negotiating contracts, wheedling our suppliers into better terms, or talking to our investors. It takes a people person to do that job, and I may be a man of many talents, but that's not one of them, I'm afraid. In this business it's important to know one's strengths and one's limitations, detective, and I'm perfectly aware of mine."

"But your brother isn't doing so hot right now, wouldn't you say?"

Jared grimaced and placed his glasses back on his nose. "Cotton has one great weakness, and that's his love of women. If he could only curb his desires in that area, he could be the best CEO this company has ever had, bar none. But unfortunately…"

"That's not the case."

"No, obviously not."

"So you're not going to step up to the plate and take over as CEO?"

"Oh, no. There are people much better equipped for that role than me. And so I leave it to them to make sure that the group is led professionally and with a lot less hassle than it has been in the past. And I'll make sure that the financials are in order."

"Any ideas on who might take over from your brother?" asked Odelia.

"No idea whatsoever," said Jared, "but I can assure you that it won't be me."

I had the impression he wasn't as forthcoming as he could have been. No doubt he was much better informed than he was letting on.

"One more question, Mr. Karat," said Chase.

"Where was I two nights ago between ten and midnight? I was home with my wife. And if you call Susan, I'm sure she'll be happy to confirm my alibi. I think we had salmon mousse, before watching an episode of *Law & Order* on TV. My wife is a lawyer, and *Law & Order* is one of her guilty pleasures." He smiled. "And now if there's nothing else…"

"I don't think he did it, Max," said Dooley once we were back in the car. "He's much too nice to murder someone in such a gruesome way. And also, if he eats salmon mousse he's definitely not a vegetarian, and our killer clearly is a vegetarian."

"Or our killer is trying to make it look as if he's a vegetarian," I said.

"Then Jared might be the killer. He struck me as a very clever guy."

"Yeah, he's definitely very clever. A lot cleverer than his brother at any rate."

"So maybe he does want to become the new CEO, and is trying to get rid of Cotton."

It was a tough one, to be sure. The clever ones enjoy playing games with the police, and I had the impression that Jared was not above that kind of behavior. Then again, when he told us he had absolutely no interest in the CEO job, he struck me as sincere. He also struck me as a much nicer person than Cotton. Then again, nice people can be killers, too—especially when they decide to murder not-so-nice people like... Cotton!

CHAPTER 24

Brutus wasn't entirely sure if this mission Max had decided to send them on was appropriately suitable for two cats in his and Harriet's position. They were, after all, master sleuths in their own right, and for some reason spying on some gang of duck fans seemed below them somehow. More the work of a feline lower on the pecking order. Then again, if Gran and Scarlett had been roped into this spy business, it might be up to snuff.

In spite of her earlier protestations, Lita Fiol had decided to call a meeting of the Duck Liberation Agency or Front or whatever the hell they were called, and here they now were, all gathered in Lita's basement, with the latter waxing lyrically on all things duck.

Gran and Scarlett were doing their utmost to look interested, even though their initial excitement to take up the cause had waned to a great degree, while Brutus and Harriet had been relegated to the hefty bags both women had dragged in with them.

The official line was that duck lovers are also cat haters,

since cats and ducks are mortal enemies, so sneaking a couple of cats into a meeting of duck fans was a no-no.

And so Gran had outfitted two bags with the necessary holes for oxygen, and now here they sat, having to keep absolutely mum for however many hours this farce would last.

It all seemed so… undignified. Especially for a pair of proud cats like them.

"Pssst!" suddenly the bag next to Brutus's bag hissed.

"What!" Brutus whispered back.

"I have to tinkle!"

"You'll just have to hold it in, won't you?"

"I've been holding it in for the past hour. How much longer is this going to take?"

"Not much longer." He hoped. A pat on the bag told him that Gran had overheard their whispered conversation and wasn't in full agreement on this breach of a policy that clearly outlined that a bag, when brought into a meeting, is not supposed to start talking!

"So are we all clear?" asked Lita. "We're very close to our goal now, people. One last push and I think we'll finally be able to get the public onside and show them what a horrible practice they've been perpetuating by consuming the flesh of the duck."

"Hear, hear!" a few other members of the DLF called out, stomping their feet for good measure. It made Brutus fear for his life, since those feet felt too close for comfort.

He now realized how James Bond must feel when sneaking around Blofeld's lair. Of course James Bond always had some pretty blonde traipsing along, but then Brutus had Harriet by his side, which practically amounted to the same thing.

"What about the death of Eric Blandine?" asked one member.

"What about it?" Lita returned, a little frostily.

"Well, the police seem to think it was one of us, don't they?"

"Yeah, they came to my door this morning," another voice piped up. "Started accusing me of all kinds of stuff. Seemed to think I was Blandine's killer, just because I've got a poster in my window that reads 'Death to All Duck Killers!'"

"Same here," said another member. "We're under attack, Lita. We're being painted as this ragtag group of murderers and extremists. Pretty soon now they'll come for us."

"They won't come for us," Lita assured her people. "Because we know we didn't do it."

"Do we?" asked Gran. "The man was killed by removing his liver, for crying out loud."

"Yeah, it must have been a member of this group," Scarlett chimed in.

Worried murmurs rose up, before Lita cut in, "Rubbish. We all took an oath."

"I didn't take no oath," said Gran. "What oath is this?"

"The oath of nonviolence. We want to save the ducks the Gandhi way. And that means we don't raise a finger against the enemy, and we most definitely do not go out and murder them."

"At any rate, whoever killed Eric Blandine messed up, didn't they?" a member said. "They should have killed Cotton Karat instead!"

"Do you think 'they' will try again?" asked Gran.

"How should I know?" that same voice returned. "I didn't do it."

"Then who did?" Gran asked. "It must be one of us, right?"

Silence reigned for a moment, then another round of recriminations started. Clearly everyone thought that one of this lot had killed Mr. Blandine, but no one was prepared to own up to it.

"You know what?" Gran finally cut in. "I know this might not be a politically correct thing to say, but as far as I'm concerned, whoever killed Eric Blandine deserves a medal. They've done something heroic for the duck cause. An eye for an eye is what I say!"

"Or a liver for a liver," Scarlett quipped, earning herself a mild smattering of laughter.

"Enough!" suddenly Lita cried, and judging from a chair that was scraped back, their fearless leader had risen to her feet. "This is no way to talk about that poor man. Have we forgotten why we started this protest? Because we cherish life! Not only human life but mallard life, too! And I'm sorry, Mrs. Muffin, but I can't condone this kind of statement!"

"What did I do?" asked Gran.

"I'm sorry, but you can't be a member of the Duck Liberation Front any longer."

"You're firing me?!" Gran cried.

"That's right. Your membership has been revoked. Now please leave. And that goes for you, too, Miss Canyon."

"But…"

"I really can't hold it in any longer, sweetums," Harriet said. "Here goes nothing."

"Mrs. Muffin?" Lita suddenly said. "Why is your bag leaking?"

"There's something moving in there," another voice cried out.

Suddenly Brutus was unceremoniously lifted up, bag and all, and moments later oxygen was finally restored to him. Though when he found himself staring at three hostile faces hovering over him, his equanimity quickly left him.

"Cats!" Lita cried. "You brought cats in here!"

"Traitors!" one of her followers screamed. "Get them!"

"Run for your lives!" suddenly Gran yelled.

And then Brutus found himself running like the wind,

Harriet hot on his trail, with the two older ladies surprisingly quick off the mark and coming right behind them.

"Enemies of the duck!" Lita was shouting. "They're all enemies of the duck!"

Up the stairs it went, through a long, dark corridor, and then finally out the front door. And even then the foursome didn't stop to catch their breath. Those duck people might pride themselves in all of that Gandhian nonviolence guff, but they seemed pretty violent to Brutus! In fact he had a strong suspicion that if they finally managed to get their hands on them, their livers wouldn't stand a chance!

Finally they rounded a corner, and Gran paused to take a breather.

"I think…" she panted heavily. "We… lost… them." She was resting her hands on her knees and sucking in big gulps of air. "Jeez! These people are completely screwy!"

"They love ducks more than they love people, that's for sure," Scarlett chimed in. She, too, looked a little the worse for wear.

"I'm sorry, Gran," said Harriet. "But I really couldn't hold it in anymore."

"That's all right, honey," said Gran. "That meeting went on a lot longer than I thought."

"I actually had to tinkle myself," said Scarlett.

"So what did we learn?" asked Brutus. "That the duck people killed Eric Blandine?"

"If I were a betting woman," said Gran, "which I'm not, I'd put good money on it."

"You'd put good money on what?" asked Scarlett.

"You really have to learn my cats' lingo," said Gran.

"I've tried, all right! It's no good. It all sounds like gibberish to me."

"Anyway. I think we've got enough here to get an arrest,

don't you think?" said Gran, and took out her phone and clicked on the 'Stop' button on her recording app.

"Did you get all of it?" asked Scarlett.

"I sure did," said Gran proudly. She gave Harriet and Brutus a cheerful glance. "We did good tonight, you guys. James Bond doesn't come anywhere near it. Our undercover mission was a roaring success!"

"And we even got to keep our livers!" Brutus added.

"Take that, Max," Harriet said with a wink.

Max might be Hampton Cove's super sleuth, but it was doubtful he'd have been able to pull off a daring stunt like this!

CHAPTER 25

We were in Uncle Alec's office, discussing the case and trying to come up with a strategy on how to move forward. Chase and Odelia were studying their notes while Uncle Alec had taken a phone call... from his mother!

"Uh-huh," he was saying. "Uh-huh, uh-huh, uh-huh. No way." Finally he hung up, and sat staring before him for a moment, then finally looked up. "My mom went undercover in the Duck Liberation Front. Did you know anything about this?"

"Yeah, she told us," said Odelia.

"Well, looks like she changed her mind," said Odelia's uncle. "She and Scarlett were just driven out of a meeting and pursued half a block, just because they brought in Harriet and Brutus, concealed in a pair of bags." He tugged at his bulbous nose. "Why would they take cats to a meeting of duck fans? That doesn't make any sense."

"I'm afraid that's my fault," I piped up. "I suggested that Brutus and Harriet keep a close eye on Lita's outfit. Find out what they're up to."

Odelia relayed my words to the others and Uncle Alec

frowned. "Ma is also convinced that one of Lita's group is behind the murder of Eric Blandine. Though when she said that whoever killed Blandine deserves a medal, Lita kicked her and Scarlett out of the group."

"Yeah, Lita is in the clear," said Chase. "She and Tobias Pushman are an item, and they were together the night Eric was killed."

"Okay," said Uncle Alec, clapping his hands. "Give me a rundown of the case. What have we got so far?"

"Well, if we assume that the killer was actually targeting Cotton and not Eric," said Odelia, "then we're looking for a person or persons who held a grudge against Cotton."

"And the list of people who hated Cotton is long," Chase warned. "There's his ex-wife Dawn, who wasn't happy when Cotton left her for a younger woman, though she was with her daughter Inari that night, or so they claim. There's Inari herself, of course, who can't have liked the fact that her dad hurt her mom. Then there's Diedrich, the family patriarch, who's seriously displeased with his son's romantic shenanigans that have caused perhaps irreparable harm to the Karat Group. And of course there's Cotton's younger brother Jared, who claims he's not interested in taking over as CEO, but who could be lying."

"Alibis?" asked the Chief.

"Diedrich was home alone—his wife died a couple of years ago. Though there are servants, Diedrich could easily have snuck out and killed Eric Blandine."

"He didn't know about this whole switcheroo business?"

"Oh, yes, he did. It was Tobias's idea, but they worked it out together, hoping to save the company."

"What about the brother? What's his story?"

"Home with his wife Susan. And yes, I checked and Susan confirmed his account."

"Okay, so what we're left with is these duck nutters

and..." The Chief grabbed for his reading glasses, which were perched atop his head. "Elvis Diamond? Who's he?"

"Major shareholder of the Karat Group," said Odelia. "Stands to lose the most if Cotton keeps up his losing streak."

"Right. And you mentioned something about a competing farmer?"

"Zak Lemanowicz," said Chase, nodding. "He used to be one of the Karat Group's suppliers, until they decided to switch to Merle Poltorak. According to several people I spoke to Mr. Lemanowicz is one very unhappy duck farmer."

"Okay, so you better have a chat with both this Diamond character and the duck farmer. Now how about this supermodel Cotton was dating? Did you check her alibi?"

"We did," said Chase. "She was indeed in a conference call with the *Vogue* people. They're featuring her for the twentieth time and they're doing something special."

"So that's a bust, too," said the Chief, mussing up his thinning mane so he momentarily looked like a crazy scientist. Then he carefully flattened it again against his skull. "Right! Well, off you go, then. And bring me something good this time. I want results, people—results!" And to emphasize his words, he glared in my direction for some reason.

I gave him my best smile, which was completely lost on him, then we all skedaddled.

"Tough case," said Dooley as we walked out. "Everybody seems to have an alibi. It's not fair, Max. Why do they all have an alibi?"

"Because they're all innocent?" I suggested.

"But innocent people don't have alibis, Max. Innocent people don't bother with that kind of stuff. They simply go about their lives and don't care if a person is murdered or not. But this lot, they all have carefully constructed alibis! Conference calls, and wives and husbands and television programs they were watching..." He frowned. "How do we know that Dawn and Inari Karat were watching *Bedazzled*? They could be making it up."

"Of course," I said. "Just like Jared's wife Susan could be making it up. Or Tobias and Lita Fiol. All these people giving one another alibis, it's all highly suspect, Dooley."

He gave me a suspicious look, figuring I was probably being sarcastic. But I wasn't. It was all very flimsy. A wife giving her husband an alibi. A boyfriend giving his girlfriend an alibi. Or a mother and daughter. How could you be sure they were telling the truth? You simply couldn't! The only one who had a solid alibi was Ebony Pilay. Those *Vogue* people weren't going to lie for her sake, now were they? Though of course they might. She was, after all, a highly successful and important model, and they were all good friends.

And friends have been known to lie to protect people, haven't they?

"I think it's the duck people," said Dooley as we all got into the car. "One of them must have snapped. It happens all the time. They're all peaceful and loving and hugging ducks and then all of a sudden something fizzles in their brain and they go completely cuckoo."

"It's possible," I allowed. Though somehow it all seemed too... convenient for my taste. Too easy. As if the killer was desperately trying to point to Lita's outfit. I mean, who in their right mind would murder a person in such a way that made it obvious that you were to blame? The duck people might be a little nutty, but surely they weren't idiots?

Of course chasing two cats through the streets wasn't exactly the hallmark of a sound mind...

CHAPTER 26

Elvis Diamond happened to live in the same apartment complex as Ebony Pilay, so we already knew the way when we arrived there. The man had secured himself a loft at the top of the building, which comprised the entire floor. He even had a private elevator so he wouldn't have to breathe the same air as those less fortunate than himself.

Mr. Diamond was a man in his mid-forties, with an excellent taste in clothes. He had a stylish beard thing going, and wore dark glasses even though we were inside. Maybe he had a problem with his eyes, or else he just thought he looked cool. Like a rock star.

"So what can I do for you?" he said, smiling beneficently as if granting us a favor.

"You're the major shareholder of the Karat Group?" asked Chase.

"That's right. After the family, of course. They still own the majority of stock."

"So with the price of the stock dropping, you must have lost a great deal of money?"

He shrugged. "Your experienced investor learns to take these vicissitudes in stride."

"A fifty percent drop in price is a big chunk of change. You must have been furious."

"I can assure you that I wasn't. And I'm sure that the stock price will rise again. The fundamentals of the Karat Group are sound. Nothing has changed on that front." He made a slight gesture. "It's an emotional response to an unfortunate lapse of judgment on Cotton's part. But nothing that won't rectify itself in the long run. And make no mistake: I'm in this for the long haul. I'm not a day trader, in and out looking to make a quick buck. I invest in the Karat Group because I believe in the long-term prospects of the group."

"Still, it must have been a bad day for you when Cotton managed to singlehandedly sink the stock and cause you to lose millions."

The man gave us a placid smile. "Is there a point to this, detective?"

"I'm curious to know where you were on the night that Eric Blandine was killed. Let's say between ten and midnight?"

"I was here."

"Alone?"

"Yes."

"So no one can vouch for you?"

"I'm afraid not."

And while Chase and Mr. Diamond squared off, Dooley and I decided to wander off and look for a bite to eat. We'd discovered that Elvis Diamond owned a pet, and if my nose wasn't deceiving me, that pet was a cat, and since the investor seemed like a very rich man, we were both anxious to see what kind of kibble all of that money would buy.

We ambled into the kitchen, just to have a quick look-see,

you see, when we came upon a smallish gray cat, who looked a lot like Dooley.

"Hey there," I said when we laid eyes on her. "Mind if we take a look around?"

The cat, who seemed a little shy, gave us a keen look from beneath long lashes. "I'm sorry, but who are you?"

"My name is Max and this is Dooley," I said, making the necessary introductions. But if I'd expected to be invited to partake in her meals, I was very much mistaken.

"This is private property," she said. "My private property. So I'm going to have to ask you to leave."

"We were invited here," I said, taken aback by this sudden vehemence. "Our humans are detectives, you see, and they're here to talk to your human." Or at least I assumed Elvis Diamond was her human. "So technically we're valued guests here."

"What's your name?" asked Dooley.

The cat continued to look a little shy, though her words belied that stance. "Priscilla," she said. "Though Elvis calls me Pris." She eyed Dooley with unveiled curiosity. "You look familiar somehow. Have we met before?"

"I don't think so," said Dooley. "I'm sure I'd remember."

The cat simpered a little at this, and I could tell that Dooley was doing a good job at breaking the ice. A much better job than I was doing, at any rate. So I decided to keep my trap shut. Some cats are intimidated when they come into contact with a, let's say, big cat like me. They see my heft and bulk and think I'm probably some bruiser type. Whereas I'm as far removed from the bruiser type as you can get. A pussycat, really, that's me.

"So do you eat meat?" asked Dooley.

"Of course, silly," said Pris. "What cat doesn't?"

"I don't," said Dooley. "You see, I'm a vegetarian."

This was news to me, but I refrained from comment.

"A vegetarian!" Pris cried, clearly amused. "You're pulling my paw."

"No, I'm not. I've seen how they treat ducks, and it's not pretty."

"You've met a duck, have you?"

"Yes, up close and in person. His name was Fred, and he wasn't happy, there in his little cage, being fattened up so he could be served up as food for some meat eater." These last words were spoken with a touch of scorn, as befitting your true vegetarian.

"Well, I don't know about that," said Pris. "You see, I've never set paw outside of this apartment. So I've never met a duck, or any other living creature, really."

"Oh, you poor thing!" Dooley cried with heartfelt pity.

"It's all right," said Pris. "You get used to the cloistered life. And it's not as if I can complain, really. Elvis really spoils me. The best food, and the best toys. And it is pretty dangerous out there, as he keeps reminding me. So it's probably all for the best."

"It can get dangerous out there," Dooley agreed. "Two friends of ours were chased by duck people today. They almost didn't make it out alive."

"What are duck people?" asked Pris, interested.

"People who love ducks," Dooley explained.

Pris laughed. "You're so funny, Dooley."

Meanwhile, I'd engaged in a close inspection of the kitchen, and had hit upon the jackpot: three bowls filled with the most delicious food a cat can hope to find. I was salivating, and my tummy was rumbling, reminding me it was past my feed time.

"Could I trouble you for a few nuggets of kibble?" I asked finally.

"Go ahead," said Pris. "Eat as much as you like."

She didn't need to tell me twice, and for the next couple

of minutes I was dead to the world as I gobbled up as much as I could in as short a space of time as I could manage.

When Pris finally returned her attention to me, she laughed an incredulous laugh. "How did you do that?!" she cried.

I gave her a guilty look. "Too much?"

"No, it's fine. I just wonder where you put it. Usually a bowl like that is enough to last me three days."

"That's because you don't get out much," I said.

"It's also because Max is much bigger than you," said Dooley reverently. "He's probably five times your size, Pris, so he also needs to eat five times as much as you."

"Hey," I said. "I'm not five times her size."

They both studied me for a moment, then Pris said, "No, you're right. You're probably ten times my size."

God. Everyone's a critic.

"Is it true that your human didn't leave the apartment two nights ago?" I asked, deciding to make sure this visit paid off in more ways than could be measured in kibble.

"Oh, absolutely," said Pris. "Elvis rarely leaves the apartment."

"And is it true that he didn't mind one bit that Cotton Karat lost him half his investment?"

"Max!" said Dooley. "You can't interrogate Pris like that. She's not a suspect."

"I'm sorry," I murmured. I guess that nasty crack about my weight still stung.

"But Max has a point," Dooley said. "You see, a man was murdered, and we're trying to find out who did it. I personally think it was the duck people, but Max thinks that's too obvious. So now we're trying to figure out where everyone was when this man was killed, and if they had a good motive for killing him."

"Well... Elvis has been in a bad mood for the past couple

of days," said Pris. "He watched something on television the other day, and it must have upset him a great deal, for he threw his remote across the room, and then he spent the rest of the day on the phone shouting at people. He seemed very anxious to get rid of a man named Cotton and to get a man named Jared to take his place. In fact he talked to this Jared person a lot."

"Jared Karat, huh?" I said, exchanging a knowing glance with Dooley. "Interesting."

"You really shouldn't stop eating meat, Dooley," said Pris now. "It's not good for you. Us cats can't afford to be vegetarians, you know. In fact we might die if we go that route."

"Die!" Dooley cried, fully aghast.

"Of course. Cats are carnivores, Dooley. We need meat. If we don't, well, it's the end."

"The end! Oh, no!"

"Oh, sweet Dooley, I didn't mean to upset you," said Pris, as she nudged my friend. "But it's true. Whoever told you to become a vegetarian was doing you a disservice."

Dooley directed a look at me, and Pris gasped in shock. "You told him! But Max—you could have killed him!"

"What are you talking about? I didn't tell him to become a vegetarian!" I said.

"But you didn't tell me not to become one either," Dooley pointed out.

"I did! I told you exactly the same thing Pris is telling you right now!"

"No, you didn't."

"I did—I really did!"

"Oh, Max. You're not a good friend to Dooley, are you?" said Pris, tsk-tsking lightly.

For crying out loud! What was the world coming to, if cats were going to distort my words! But since I had an urgent message for Odelia, I decided not to argue my point,

PURRFECT DOUBLE

but to return to the living room, where Chase and Mr. Diamond were still duking it out.

"You can't come in here and bully me, detective," Elvis was saying.

"I'm not bullying you!" Chase said.

I quickly snuck up to Odelia and whispered a few words into her ear. She smiled and gave me a grateful pat on the head. At least one person in this apartment still liked me.

"Mr. Diamond," said Odelia. "Elvis. Isn't it true that you hated Cotton sinking your stock and spent all day on the phone with Jared, trying to convince him to take over as CEO?"

Elvis's jaw dropped at this. "How did you…"

"I have my sources," said Odelia with a tight smile. "But it's true, isn't it?"

Elvis blinked, then finally inclined his head. "Yes, it's true. I've never been a big fan of Cotton. The man's all flash and glib sales talk. But when it comes down to business, he's as inept as they come. He doesn't care about the group. All he cares about is himself and the women he likes to surround himself with. He's bad news and has proven a disaster as CEO. So yes, I wanted Jared to take over from his brother. And if he didn't, I told Diedrich I'd unload every last piece of stock I owned. Cut my losses and bail." He grimaced. "I don't have to tell you that didn't go down well. In fact it was probably the main reason they suddenly bundled Cotton into a car and shipped him off to that rehab facility."

"Jared wasn't aware of that, was he?"

"Oh, of course he was. Do you really think Tobias Pushman would pull a stunt like that all on his own? You can't whisk off the CEO of one of the biggest companies in this country without the go-ahead of the rest of the management team—or the man's family."

"So if Cotton's family knew that Eric Blandine was a lookalike…" said Chase.

"… they had absolutely no reason to kill him," Odelia completed the sentence.

"And neither did I," said Elvis. "Since I knew about the switch from the start."

"Right," said Chase, sounding disappointed.

"Did you get Jared to agree to take his brother's place?" asked Odelia.

Elvis sighed. "It's not as simple as you think. A lot of investors don't like Jared."

"And why is that?"

"Jared botched an important deal a couple of years ago. This was when Diedrich was still CEO. Both brothers were vying for his position, and as a test Diedrich tasked them with reeling in two big clients. Cotton pulled it off with flying colors, but Jared managed to make a total mess of things. He'd flown off to China for some final negotiations and when he got there set the meeting in a brothel of all places. The Chinese delegation was rightly outraged and the deal ended up in the toilet. Rumor had it that it was actually Cotton who'd arranged that meeting place."

"To sabotage his brother," said Chase.

"Exactly. One month later Cotton was announced as the new CEO and Jared as CFO."

"But Jared told us he has absolutely no interest in being CEO," said Odelia. "Never has."

"Pardon my French, but then he fed you a lot of crap, Mrs. Kingsley. Jared's always wanted to follow in his father's footsteps. And between you and me, he'd make a much better CEO than Cotton. Which is why I've been trying to persuade Diedrich to give him another chance. And with Cotton making an absolute shambles of things, he just might."

CHAPTER 27

"What else did Pris tell you?" I asked once we were back in the car.

"Oh, just that I have to be my own cat from now on, and not listen to your bad advice."

"Bad advice! I was the one who told you that not eating meat will kill you!"

"No, you didn't. You urged me on. Made me go down a dangerous road."

"Oh, for crying out loud."

"She also told me that I should never listen to a cat who's as clearly obese as you."

"I'm not obese," I said frostily. "I've told you this a hundred times. I'm big-boned."

"I'm sorry, Max, but what Pris said really resonated with me. I think from now on I'm going to have to keep my own counsel."

"What does that even mean!"

"I means," said my best friend, "that I don't need your advice anymore." And then he ostentatiously turned his back on me and proceeded to ignore me for the rest of the ride.

Jared didn't look happy when we paid him a second visit in one day. "I think I've said all I have to say," he grumbled when we walked in. "And if you want to speak to me you'd better get in touch with my lawyers."

"We just had a chat with Elvis Diamond," said Chase, ignoring the man's outburst and planting his hands on his desk. "And he told us that you've been conspiring with him to replace your brother as CEO. So all that nonsense you gave us about not being a people person and not having any interest in being CEO? I'm afraid you've wasted your breath."

Jared stared at the cop, eyes glittering, then finally relented. "All right, so I've been in negotiation with Elvis. We had to do something. My dad is either too blind or too stubborn to see it, but Cotton is destroying this company. Another six months with him in charge and stock will be trading at cents on the dollar! So we had to act now to save us."

"And what did your dad say?"

"He's coming around to our point of view."

"And Cotton? What part does he play in all this?"

Jared looked away. "Cotton still has a part to play. But not as CEO."

"So you'll be replacing him, is that it? When was this decided?"

"We're going to announce it at the next conference call."

"You're a real piece of work, aren't you, Jared?" said Chase.

"I couldn't tell you! In fact I'd appreciate it if you kept this to yourselves. It's highly sensitive information that could have an enormous impact on the market. We have to tread very carefully, and make sure the transition goes off without a hitch this time."

"Is it true that your brother sabotaged your first bid for leadership?" asked Odelia.

Jared laughed as he dragged his fingers through his hair. "Elvis has really opened up, hasn't he? Had a real heart-to-heart with you two? What is this? His Oprah moment?"

"The truth this time, Jared," said Chase. "At least if you remember the meaning of the word."

"Okay, all right! Yes, Cotton sabotaged my first bid for CEO, and I've hated him for it ever since. Happy now?"

"So you decided to take revenge by having him evicted from his office this time."

"No! Well, yes, in a way, I guess. But not out of spite. In the interest of the company."

"Of course," said Chase. "Everything you do is in the best interests of the company."

"You don't understand, detective."

"So enlighten me."

"I've been forced to sit here and watch our profits dwindle year after year, through the sheer ineptitude of my brother. Because he can't be bothered to keep his eye on the ball. Did you know that he alienated our best foie gras supplier and now we're forced to sell an inferior product? And don't think for a minute that the customer doesn't notice, because he does."

"This alienated supplier wouldn't be Zak Lemanowicz, by any chance?"

Jared looked surprised. "How did you…"

"I'm wondering, Mr. Karat," said Chase, taking a seat on the edge of the man's desk and picking up a perpetuum mobile that sat there. It consisted of balls suspended from strings, and when you hit one ball, it hit the next, and so on until the whole thing reversed. He now let drop the first ball. "I'm wondering whether your desire to save the company was so strong that you decided to kill Eric Blandine and send a clear message to your brother: back off or you're next."

Jared swallowed. "I already told you: I was home with my wife Susan."

"Wives have been known to lie to protect their husbands."

"Oh, for heaven's sake, man. Do you really believe I'd drag the group through a murder inquiry? It's bad enough that Cotton tanked the stock with his outrageous behavior, but this murder business has really put us on the spot. We all thought we could get away with Cotton being tucked away for the time being, and now it's completely blown up in our faces." He snatched the mobile from Chase's hands and replaced it on his desk. "Can't you see that Blandine's murder is the last thing I need? The last thing this company needs!"

"You have to admit it's handy if you want to put pressure on Cotton and your dad."

"Get out," said Jared, whose face had taken on a dangerously dark color. "And next time you want to talk to me—you better call my lawyer first!"

Looks like we'd outstayed our welcome, and so we left.

CHAPTER 28

The duck farm that Mr. Lemanowicz presided over was not a big operation, but it still housed a couple of thousand ducks. Less than the place where Eric Blandine had met a sticky end, but nevertheless a lot of ducks to contend with. Lita Fiol would have felt right at home there, I imagined, and so would her duck-loving, cat-hating buddies.

We found Zak Lemanowicz in one of the big barns, where he was dumping what looked like slop into large rubber bowls. The ducks eagerly came waddling up and tucked in. So the slop might actually have been food. Not to my taste, though. Then again, as already indicated, I'm probably spoiled.

"Mr. Lemanowicz," said Chase, walking up to the man. The farmer was dressed like one would expect: in green coveralls, rubber boots and a leathery face. "A word, please, sir?" And since he was holding up his badge, he made it obvious that his question was more in the nature of an order, not a request.

"What do you want?" the farmer grunted.

"Just a couple of questions," said Odelia in more kindly tones.

"It's always just a couple of questions," the man grumbled.

"You used to be the Karat Group's main supplier of foie gras?" asked Odelia.

"I was, until Cotton decided he could get a better deal and took his business elsewhere."

"To Merle Poltorak."

"I trained Merle. He was a farmhand here for years. When he went into business for himself I even helped set him up. And that's how he repaid me for my kindness: by snatching my biggest client and promising him he could supply the same product for half the price. Taught me a lesson right there."

"According to Jared Karat Merle delivers an inferior product?"

"Of course he does. Do you really think I was overcharging the Karats? You can't lower your price and expect the same quality. And now I hear people are complaining that Karat foie gras isn't what it used to be. Big surprise!"

"Can I ask you where you were two nights ago, Zak?"

"Right here at the farm. Even though it's not the same operation it used to be, I still have my customers, and I still put in a lot of hours to keep them happy."

Odelia gave me and Dooley a surreptitious nod of the head, and so we trod off, looking for witnesses who could verify Zak's statement.

We found plenty of those in the stable, and when we approached the first one, it struck me how much happier Zak's ducks looked compared to Merle's.

"These ducks look so happy, Max," said Dooley, apparently having forgotten he wasn't speaking to me anymore.

"That's because they get to roam around freely," I said.

"Instead of being boxed up in a small cage like at the other place."

"Hi, Mr. Duck," said Dooley, addressing the first duck who'd give us the time of day. The others were all still tucking into the slop Zak had fed them. "Can we ask you a couple of questions, please?"

"Oh, absolutely," said the duck, approaching us with a kindly expression on his face. "Ask away."

"Do you like it here, sir?" asked Dooley. Not exactly a question I would have asked, but since Odelia and Chase were still deep in conversation with the duck farmer, we had plenty of time to get to the nub of our query.

"Oh, sure," said the duck. "What's not to like? I have all my friends here, plenty of food, fresh air, and Zak is such a great guy. He treats us like family, you know."

"But… you do know what kind of place this is, don't you?" said Dooley delicately.

The duck laughed at this. "You mean, at the end of the ride we get to go the way of the dodo?"

"Well, yes," said Dooley.

"I know, sweet cheeks," said the duck. "But only when we're good and ready to go."

"So… you get to live a long life here?" asked Dooley, perking up.

"Of course! We don't have to go before our time, young 'un. And that's what makes this place special. And also, we get to spend plenty of time outside—out of this stable."

We both glanced to the grassy meadows nearby, and saw ducks waddling around there, and even spend time in the pond. Not a bad way to live, all in all.

"Someone recently advised me to become a vegetarian," said Dooley, giving me a bit of side-eye at this point, and causing me to roll my own eyes in exasperation. "But then someone else told me this is a bad idea, since cats aren't supposed to be vegetarians."

"Oh, sweetie, who tricked you into believing cats can be vegetarians!"

Dooley turned a baleful eye on me.

"It wasn't me!" I cried.

"What do you eat, Mr. Duck?"

"Just call me Dave," said the duck. "Well, I eat most everything. Fish eggs, small fish, worms, snails, insects, frogs, slugs, tadpoles, mollusks…" He smiled. "I'm not choosy."

"So they're not force-feeding you?" I asked.

"Most certainly not! Imagine that!"

"Most foie gras is produced by shoving a pipe down a duck's throat and overfeeding them," I pointed out.

"That's just gross!" Dave cried. "No, Zak doesn't do that, thank God."

We turned to Zak. Looked like he was one of the good guys.

"Okay, so this is important, Dave," I said. "Where was Zak two nights ago?"

"Well, right here, of course," said Dave. "Mucking out the stables as usual."

"That's great news," said Dooley. "That means that Zak didn't kill Eric."

"Who's Eric?"

"He's a man who was killed over in another duck farm," I explained.

"Bad business, huh? You won't find that kind of thing going on here."

And then he went off foraging some more food. That liver didn't feed itself.

We'd joined Odelia again when all of a sudden a familiar figure walked in. It was none other than… Ebony Pilay!

"Hey, honey," the supermodel said, teetering on high heels

and sidestepping a piece of duck dung. She pressed a quick kiss to Zak's cheek and gave Odelia and Chase a look of amusement. "What's wrong, detective? You look like you've seen a ghost."

"You two know each other?" asked Chase.

"Ebony is my ex-wife," Zak explained. "Though we're just friends now."

Chase had to reel in his jaw. Now this was a development he hadn't expected.

CHAPTER 29

"When-when did you say you divorced?" asked Chase, still trying to collect himself.

"I didn't say," said Ebony with a smile. "You're surprised that a duck farmer would marry a model, is that it?"

"Well... yes," Chase admitted.

"It's not that hard to imagine. Zak is a very sweet man, and I wasn't always a model."

It was a little hard to see the attraction. Then again, Zak did have a sort of rugged charm, I guess. And even though his face was weather-beaten, he was probably younger than what we'd pegged him. Perhaps he was even Ebony's age, since she was probably older than she looked.

"We divorced about ten years ago," said Zak, "but we've stayed friends, which can't be said about all couples, I guess." He smiled at his former wife. "Ebony wanted to pursue a different path from being a duck farmer's wife, and even though I was as sore as a gumboil at the time, I can see now that she made the right decision. She did well for herself."

"Well!" said Ebony with a laugh. "That's probably the understatement of the century."

"Okay, so you did very well," Zak amended his earlier statement.

"So let me get this straight," said Chase. "First Cotton Karat stole your wife, and then he canceled your contract? You must hate that man a lot, Mr. Lemanowicz."

"I only met Cotton a couple of months ago," said Ebony, "so Cotton didn't 'steal' me from anyone. But that contract… that did rankle, didn't it?"

"I already admitted I was unhappy about that," Zak grumbled. "But to murder a man over a contract, that's taking things too far."

"Zak is not a killer, detective. In fact the man couldn't hurt a fly."

"He does treat his ducks very well," Dooley piped up.

Odelia smiled down in our direction. "We'll check your alibi," she said, "but from where I'm standing I'm inclined to believe you, Zak."

Chase had picked up on the interaction between his wife and her cats, and he emitted a small groan of frustration. Another person who had looked so good for the murder, and another alibi that seemed rock solid.

"You and Cotton, that's definitely over?" asked Odelia now.

Ebony grinned. "Is this also part of the inquiry, Mrs. Kingsley?"

"No, this is purely for my own interest," Odelia admitted.

"Yeah, we're over. He called me this morning, said it wasn't him who sent me that text, but even so, these last couple of days have taught me that Cotton isn't the man for me. The guy is a womanizer of the purest water. And even though all we did was have some fun, I'm starting to see that maybe I'm too old for that kind of thing." She gave her ex-husband an affectionate look. "Sometimes it takes losing something before you realize how important it was to you all along."

"Looks like they might get back together again, Max," said Dooley, once again having forgotten all about the grudge he was harboring toward me. "Isn't that sweet?"

"The supermodel and the duck farmer. Almost sounds like a Hallmark romance," I said.

And since there was nothing more for us to learn there, we repaired to the car.

"And maybe he'll even get his contract with the Karat Group back," Dooley pointed out.

"Getting his wife back and his contract. It's a good day for Zak Lemanowicz," I said as we climbed onto the backseat.

Moments later, we were cruising along. "So what now?" asked Odelia.

"Now I don't know anymore," said Chase. "Zak obviously alibied out. And same thing goes for Elvis Diamond. Both of those alibis sussed out by your cats, I might add."

"Whatever it takes to get to the truth..." She thought for a moment. "Did you ever find out how Eric Blandine was lured to the farm?"

"Nope. Nothing on his phone, computer... Also no fingerprints on the package containing his liver, or the tin, or even on the card."

"This is turning into a tough case, Mr. Kingsley."

"It most certainly is, Mrs. Kingsley." He then dropped his gaze down to his wife's belly. "How are you feeling? Isn't this too stressful for you?"

"I'm fine, Chase!"

"All right, all right."

"How is the baby bump?" asked Dooley curiously, inserting himself between the two car seats to take a gander.

"The bump is fine," said Odelia with a satisfied smile as she affectionately rubbed said bump.

"Do you think the baby is going to be a vegetarian?"

Odelia chuckled. "Oh, Dooley. What kind of a question is that?"

"Just curious. Are babies carnivores, herbivores or omnivores?"

"Omnivores, I guess, like the rest of the human race."

"I've stopped being a vegetarian," said Dooley.

"That's good news," said Odelia, closing her eyes for a moment.

"Max advised me to become a vegetarian but Pris told me I could die."

"Max never told you to become a vegetarian, Dooley," said Odelia. "You came up with that silly idea all by yourself. In fact Max told you that you shouldn't become a vegetarian."

Dooley frowned. "He did?"

"Of course. Max is your friend. He doesn't want you to die."

"He doesn't?"

"Of course not. Who is this Pris, anyway?"

"Elvis Diamond's cat Priscilla."

"She's been feeding you a lot of nonsense, Dooley."

"Oh?"

"Some women are like that. They try to come between you and your best friends. They probably think it will tie you closer to them, which is nonsense, of course. All it does is alienate you from your friends and you'll end up resenting the person responsible."

"Oh," Dooley repeated, as he darted a quick look in my direction.

"Sounds like your Pris is exactly such a person."

"Okay. Thanks for the warning."

"You're welcome." She turned to me. "Have you figured it out yet, Max? Cause we're at the end of our rope here, as you can probably see."

"No, I'm afraid the whole thing is still a mystery to me."

"Thought so," she muttered. "Well, don't let me keep you. Work that big brain of yours, will you? Cause this entire case looks just about ready to fall apart around us."

Just then, her phone chimed, telling her a message had arrived. She took it out and stared at the message. It was a video, which started playing the moment she clicked on it.

"Oh, my God!" she cried. "Pull over!"

Chase pulled over, and together they watched the video. Judging from the sounds, it was something really gruesome connected to ducks, though Odelia shielded her phone so we couldn't see.

"Trust me," she said finally. "It's better that you don't see."

"There's a message," said Chase.

"'Check Lita Fiol's phone,'" Odelia read.

"I knew it!" said Chase. "They've been lying to us from the start!"

He immediately started the car again, and moments later we were zooming along, this time in the direction of the shop where Lita worked.

CHAPTER 30

Miss Fiol was behind the counter when we arrived. Chase wasted no time demanding to see her phone, and in spite of her protestations, went through her files until he found it. He then held up the phone for her to see, and the same video was played.

Her cheeks colored violently and she had to avert her eyes. Clearly the video affected her powerfully. "I got that vile thing a couple of days ago. Evidence that Merle Poltorak is a vicious butcher. Nothing less than a criminal. The way he treats those poor animals…"

"So you decided to teach him a lesson, didn't you? Him and Cotton Karat both. Somehow you lured the man you thought was Cotton to the farm and killed him there on the spot. Were you alone or was a member of your group there to help you set it up?"

"But I didn't—I couldn't!"

He was leaning over her now, his bulk crowding her as she cowered. "Admit it, Lita. You murdered Eric Blandine in cold blood, as a message for Merle and his main suppliers: the Karat Group."

"You're crazy! I was with Tobias that night. I already told you."

"You're lying, and so is Tobias. What did you tell him? That you needed him to supply you with an alibi? What lies did you feed him, Lita—or are the two of you in it together?"

"Of course not!"

"Tobias needed to get rid of Cotton one way or another. He's been scheming behind the man's back. And murdering his replacement would send a strong message to Diedrich and to Cotton both: time to bail out while you still can. Time for a new man at the helm."

"Look, I admit I was furious when I received the video, but instead of going out and murdering the man, I talked to Tobias. Asked him to drop Merle as a supplier. Go back to Zak Lemanowicz. He has perfected a production process that is absolutely humane."

"Oh, save it," said Chase harshly. "Lita Fiol, you're under arrest for the murder of Eric Blandine. You have the right to remain silent…"

A woman approached the counter. I recognized her from the last time we'd been in there. She was holding up a piece of tofu. "Can you tell me if there's fish in this, miss?"

"Shop is closed," said Chase gruffly, and then escorted Lita from the premises.

I glanced up at Odelia. "Do you really think that she's guilty?" I asked.

Odelia shrugged. "Honestly? I don't know anymore, Max."

We all went down to the station, where Lita was to be booked and fingerprinted, and interrogated more thoroughly by Chase. And since Chase had taken the car to transfer his arrestee, the rest of us walked the short distance from the Happy Bean to the precinct.

"Max?" said Dooley finally, after we'd traveled a block and a half in silence.

"Mh?" I said.

"I'm sorry."

"Sorry for what?"

I'd been thinking hard about this most startling development in the case, and Dooley's words took me out of my musings.

"That I thought you wanted to kill me by turning me into a vegetarian."

I smiled. It sounded ridiculous when he said it like that. "That's all right."

"No, it's not all right. I let myself be turned against you by a scheming cat. It's not okay."

"Don't be too hard on yourself, Dooley. What Pris said all sounded very plausible."

"I know, but still…" He was quiet for a few moments, then seemed to come to some kind of decision. "I want you to accept my resignation, Max."

"What are you talking about?"

"My resignation as your best friend. I behaved in a way no best friend should, and so I think you should find another cat to fill the position because I resign. In disgrace," he added, hanging his head.

"Being a friend is not like being a CEO, Dooley. You can't resign or even be fired."

He looked up at this. "You can't?"

"Of course not. You're my best friend because… well, just because you are."

"So… I can't be fired for bad behavior like Cotton Karat?"

"No, absolutely not. I can be upset with you for bad behavior, just like you can be upset with me if I behave badly, but I can't fire you, and you can't fire me."

"So you're upset with me, aren't you?" he said with a sad look.

"I was a little bit upset," I admitted. "But I'm fine now."

"Oh, Max—can you ever forgive me?"

"Nothing to forgive," I said magnanimously and with a broad smile.

"Not even for calling you obese?"

My smile faltered somewhat. "How many times, Dooley! I'm not obese!"

Now it was his turn to smile. "I knew it. You still love me, don't you? Otherwise you wouldn't get mad with me." And to show me he meant what he said, he gave me a tight hug that almost choked me. Not to mention that he did it in full view of the whole street, which contained a lot of our feline friends, who all smirked when they saw this public display of affection!

"All right, all right!" I said finally, as I tried to wriggle myself out of his embrace.

"I'm so glad we're friends again, Max," he said as he practically skipped beside me.

"Me, too," I said.

"I won't let any woman come between us again."

"Mind that you don't."

"Though she was pretty, wasn't she, Pris?"

"Very pretty," I agreed.

"Too bad she lives with that investor. He's a cold one, Max. Only thing that matters to him is his bottom."

"Bottom line, you mean."

"No, Pris told me that Elvis is very concerned with his bottom. Studies it in the mirror all the time, and does all kinds of exercises to make it look as tight as possible."

I suppressed a shiver. Imagine having to live with a man who won't let you out of the apartment, and is obsessed with his own bottom. No wonder Pris was the way she was.

"So the case is closed now, is it?"

"Yeah, I guess it is."

He studied me for a moment. "Then why do you look so sad, Max?"

"I don't look sad."

"Yes, you do. It's not that you're still angry with me, are you?"

"No, Dooley. I'm not still angry with you. But I am not fully convinced that Lita is Eric Blandine's killer, that's for sure."

"So we'll just keep on looking, shall we?"

I smiled. "You okay with that, buddy?"

"Absolutely. It's what I like best, you know."

"What is?"

"This! Sleuthing together."

I have to admit his words touched a chord.

How could they not? It's what I like best, too.

CHAPTER 31

That evening, Gran was in charge of the cooking for a change. We were all gathered in Marge and Tex's backyard, the entire family seated around the big table, but when the food finally came out, instead of shiny eyes and happy faces, mouths sagged and mutterings of disappointment could be heard. Not too loud, mind you, since Gran doesn't take criticism well.

"What's this?" asked Scarlett as she stared into her dish.

"Tofu," said Gran proudly.

"It looks like a piece of cardboard," said Scarlett, who's probably the only person in the world who's not afraid of Gran's acerbic wit. "And what's that white goo?"

"That's tofu sauce."

"It looks like paint." She took a bite. "It also tastes like paint."

"And how would you know what paint tastes like?"

"I know it tastes like crap, and that's exactly what this is. What happened to the roast beef you promised me?"

"Meat is murder, Scarlett. We're all vegetarians from now on."

"You may be a vegetarian, but I'm not."

"So you want to keep murdering the planet, do you?"

"No, but I do want some regular food." She pushed her plate away. "And this is not it."

"Oh, you ungrateful—"

But Scarlett held up her hand. "Save it, Vesta. We both know you're not the one who supplied this spread. For that we have Marge and Tex to thank. And what a waste of money it was." She smiled a gracious smile to her hosts, who sat looking a little stiff and frosty, and jabbed at their meal with expressions that told all. Even Uncle Alec and Charlene Butterwick were uncharacteristically quiet while the tofu war raged on.

For a moment, Gran and Scarlett continued to be locked in a staring contest, then finally Gran relented. "Maybe you're right," she said. "It does taste like cardboard, doesn't it? I bought it yesterday at Lita's store, and once I bought it, it seemed like a pity to throw it out."

"There's nothing wrong with tofu," finally said Marge. "It's the way you prepare it that makes all the difference. She got up and started collecting plates. "Now why don't you let me give it a try?"

"Would you?" asked Gran, almost piteously. "I don't know what happened but I just can't seem to make it edible."

"Come on, Ma," said Marge. "Let's give it our best shot."

And they both disappeared into the house.

Uncle Alec visibly relaxed, and so did the others. The prospect of having to eat the inedible and pretend to like it is probably beyond any human, or every living creature, for that matter. I had to confess that when Gran dumped a piece of tofu into my bowl, I gave it one sniff and gave up.

"It's just fermented soybeans, Max," said Harriet. "It's not poison or something."

"I don't like soybeans," I told her. "Fermented or otherwise."

"So I hear Chase arrested Lita?" said Brutus. He sounded happy about it.

"Yeah, someone sent Odelia a video of ducks being manhandled, and the same video was sent to Lita a couple of days ago, so now Chase is convinced it set her off on a murder spree."

"You don't look convinced?"

"That's because I'm not."

"I wonder who sent that video to Odelia," said Dooley.

"It was sent from an anonymous number. Untraceable."

"Maybe the same person who lured Eric Blandine to his death?"

I gave my friend a nod. "That's exactly what I thought."

"So someone is framing Lita?" Harriet asked.

"Yes, it certainly looks that way."

"Pity," said Brutus. "That woman is a menace."

"She is a danger to any cat that roams these streets," Harriet agreed.

"But that doesn't make her a murderer, does it?" I said.

Finally Marge and Gran came out of the house with steaming plates of food, and this time the experiment proved a success, for the human contingent all tucked in eagerly.

Lucky for us, we didn't get to partake in the bucolic feast. Instead, Odelia slipped us some delicious chicken. It might not be kosher, but what can you do? It tastes so good.

🐾

Later that evening, I decided to wander into town. I had to think, and a nice walk would do me good. Also, Kingman frequently has the best food in town. His human runs the General Store, and keeps Kingman's bowl filled to capacity at all times. He gets his stuff from his suppliers—sometimes excellent, sometimes not so much. Like the lottery, you simply have to throw the dice and hope you're in luck.

We were in luck that night, and the kibble that Kingman gladly shared was wonderful.

"Where have you guys been all day?" asked our friend. "Wilbur is complaining that I don't eat enough." He patted his impressive belly. "But if I eat any more I'll simply burst!"

"Do you have big bones, too, Kingman?" asked Dooley.

Kingman grinned. "Absolutely. Big bones, that's me."

I saw that Wilbur was chatting with a woman. The shop was supposed to be closed, but Wilbur likes to keep it open longer sometimes for special customers.

"Does Wilbur have a new girlfriend?" I asked, eyeing the woman with interest.

"Nah. They're just friends. Though Wilbur wouldn't mind getting to know her a little better, if you ask me."

"Do you think Wilbur will ever get married and settle down, Kingman?" asked Dooley.

"What are you talking about? The guy is old. Too old to have kids. And besides, why marry? We've got a pretty great thing going here, me and Wilbur. We're like those guys in that movie. What's it called—*The Odd Couple*."

I had to smile at that. "So who's Walter Matthau and who's Jack Lemmon?"

"Wilbur's Jack, of course. Neurotic neat freak. And I'm a happy-go-lucky kind of cat, so I must be Walter."

"Yeah, I can see that," I said. The woman had left, and Wilbur grabbed a chair and came out to sit with us.

"Nice evening, fellas," he said. "Feels like a night for love."

"So don't you think Wilbur will ever get married?" asked Dooley.

"I doubt it, Dooley," said Kingman. "After all these years, the man is set in his ways, you know. Having a woman enter the picture is going to be hard for him. Someone telling him what to do, what to eat, where to sit, how to set the table and what to watch on television. It's going to be impossible. Wilbur is more like a cat than a dog: hard to train."

"So no wedding bells for Wilbur," I concluded.

Something Kingman said resonated with me, though at the moment I couldn't really put my finger on it. Not yet, at least. I decided to let it go for now. It would come to me.

"I wish I could understand what you guys talk about," said Wilbur. "Like Vesta, you know. Or Odelia or Marge. You think they could teach me?"

We all stared at the man. "You know about the big secret?" I asked. But of course Wilbur simply stared blankly back at me, then grinned.

"See? You just said something important, I can tell. And now you're expecting an answer from me. But I'm sorry, little buddy. I can't help you there."

"I think a lot of people know about your big secret, Max," said Kingman with a shrug. "It's a small town, you know. People talk."

"Well, I hope Wilbur keeps it to himself."

"And even if he doesn't—who's going to believe him?"

Kingman had a point, of course. Who would believe a story like that?

"Hey, pretty lady," said Wilbur, and when I looked up I saw he was talking to Gran.

"Can you help me out, Wilbur?" asked Gran. "I'm dying for a piece of sausage."

Wilbur's eyes went wide. "Absolutely. My place or yours?"

"Not that kind of sausage, you pervert," Gran grunted. "A real one."

"Oh," said Wilbur, sagging a little. "Yeah, take your pick," he said. "Pay me later."

Gran disappeared into the store, and moments later

returned with a nice big sausage. She was already digging her teeth into the delicacy and drew up a chair and joined us.

"Nice night," Wilbur commented.

"Mh," said Gran, busy with her mastication.

"So you ran out of food, huh? Forgot to do your shopping?"

"I decided my family are going to be vegetarians," Gran explained.

"Oh? Interesting choice."

"So I got rid of all meat products and stocked up on vegetarian stuff." She sighed. "Marge is going to kill me when she finds out. And so is Tex—and Odelia and Chase."

"You chucked out their meat products as well?" asked Wilbur with a chuckle.

"Of course! You gotta eliminate temptation. That's the whole point of the exercise."

"I bet you forgot to tell them about that?"

"Yeah, maybe I should have mentioned something."

"You think?" Wilbur asked, and guffawed loudly.

But then Gran hit him with her sausage and that was that.

It's hard to argue with a big fat sausage when it hits you right on the noggin.

CHAPTER 32

Kingman's comments had given me some food for thought. And so the moment we returned home, I enlisted Harriet and Brutus's assistance once more to help me follow a hunch. It took a little while to convince the twosome, though. They seemed to think I was leading them straight into the Duck Liberation Front's den again, subjecting them to a potentially dangerous situation once more.

"All I'm asking is to look through Eric's study," I explained. "Chances are that we'll find a second phone, or his laptop or whatever. The killer must have contacted him somehow, and we need to figure out how and who was behind that message."

"But they already checked his phone, Max," said Harriet, who is no fool.

"And his laptop," Brutus added. "And they found nothing. Zip. Zilch. Zero."

"Yes, yes, yes, I know," I said with a touch of impatience. "But there has to be something we can do."

"Maybe the killer erased the message from Eric's phone after he killed him?" Dooley suggested.

"They checked with Eric's provider," I said. "So if a message was deleted it would have been found. No, there has to be another phone—it's the only possibility. Or a second computer."

"So why don't you tell Chase so he can organize a search of the house?" asked Brutus. "It's what he does best. Chase loves to get warrants and search people's houses. It's one of the perks of his job as a cop. Snooping around in places other people don't have access to."

"Just trust me, okay? Can't you simply trust me for once?" I said.

"The last time we trusted you we were almost killed by a group of rabid duck fans," Harriet pointed out. "So excuse us for not leaping when you tell us to jump, Max."

"Okay, fine," I said finally. "I'll just do it myself then." And I stomped off in the direction of the cat flap. If they weren't going to assist me, I'd just have to fly solo on this one.

But I hadn't even entered the backyard when I heard the cat flap flap again. When I glanced back with a smile, I saw that Dooley was hurrying to catch up with me. "Wait, Max," he said. "We're an odd couple, and you can't just go off without your better half."

"Thanks, Dooley," I said, touched by this display of loyalty. I waited for a moment, fully expecting Harriet and Brutus to join us, too, but when the seconds ticked by and the cat flap stayed still, not even flapping in the breeze, I steeled my resolve and Dooley and I wended our way toward the house where Eric Blandine had lived before he was killed.

"You have to understand, Max," said Dooley. "Harriet and Brutus were almost killed out there. They're still recovering from the ordeal. They're not used to being hunted down by rabid duck people. It was a very traumatizing experience for them."

"They were never in any real danger," I grumbled, not hiding my disappointment with our friends' behavior. "Gran and Scarlett were there. They would have protected them from that frenzied mob. And besides, they might be duck fans, but they wouldn't hurt us."

"According to Harriet and Brutus they were pretty upset, Max. If they'd had pitchforks and torches they would have used them, no doubt about it. Gran said they are rascalized."

"You mean radicalized?"

"She said they value the life of a duck over the lives of other living creatures."

"That may well be true, but that doesn't explain why Harriet and Brutus would desert us."

It took us all of half an hour to reach the Blandine place. I'd hoped for easy access to the premises, but when we'd toured the house once, it became obvious there was no pet flap, no open windows on the ground floor, and no basement windows either. In other words: they weren't making it easy for us to carry out our investigation.

"Up there, Max," Dooley whispered, gesturing to an open window on the second floor.

The window definitely had potential, but how to get up there? Luckily for us Mr. Blandine had planted a sapling once upon a time, which had grown into a sizable tree. Now I'm not a big fan of the art of climbing trees, since I've had my share of close encounters with firefighters having to come to my assistance after I happened to get stuck in one, but this seemed to be the only way to carry out our nocturnal mission.

And so we went for it. First Dooley made his way up the tree, by digging his claws into the soft bark, followed by yours truly. And then it was a simple matter of balancing on a sturdy branch, hopping to the windowsill, and sneaking in.

We found ourselves in what looked like a spare bedroom,

with an unmade bed and plenty of boxes piled up high. In the corner an ironing board stood, as well as a desk, but when we subjected the latter to a closer scrutiny, we found no trace of a laptop, phone, tablet or any other electronic device.

But we weren't as easily defeated as this, and so we snuck out into the corridor, fully prepared to expand our search to the rest of the house.

And that's when we heard it: sounds of lovemaking were coming from one of the other rooms.

Dooley and I froze and shared a look of surprise. When traipsing along in the house of a woman who's just lost her husband to a terrible crime, the last thing one expects is the sound of a couple making love.

"Probably the television," Dooley opined.

"Yeah, probably," I agreed.

Now I know we should have proceeded in the opposite direction of those sounds, since only trouble could come from investigating the matter further, but then cats will be cats, and my sense of curiosity was thusly tickled that I simply had to know what was going on. Of course different people react differently to grief, but this was one method of coping with the loss of a beloved spouse that I hadn't read about in *Cosmopolitan* or *Good Housekeeping*. Even to Dr. Phil this was probably a novel approach to the agony of bereavement.

And so we found ourselves tiptoeing in the direction of the source of those sounds. A woman was moaning, a man was groaning, a mattress was squeaking and bed boards were slapping against the wall in a manner which signaled an explosion of hot passion.

My cheeks were burning underneath my fur, and from the worried glances Dooley shot in my direction as we crept ever closer to what was most probably the master bedroom, I could tell that he was as concerned with what we'd find as I was.

"We have to stop them, Max," he whispered now. "Or call the police!"

"Why?" I asked. "As far as I know there's no law against this."

"He's murdering her, Max! Or she's murdering him!"

It is of course hard to distinguish between the sounds of a couple engaged in an act of carnality and a couple trying to murder each other. Both share certain similarities, but I think I'm an old hand at recognizing the difference. Our humans are, after all, a recently married couple, and even though I prefer not to be present when they're consummating their sacred bond, I've heard enough to know that this was not an act of murder but love.

So I pushed open the door to the bedroom, tiptoed around the bed, and gasped in shock at what my keen eyes observed.

Maisie Blandine was in bed with her brother-in-law Fabrizio Blandine, and they weren't playing a game of Scrabble!

Unfortunately for us, Dooley wasn't as skilled at keeping his surprise to himself, for when he caught a good look at the surprising couple, he squealed with sincere shock.

Maisie practically jumped to the ceiling, and so did Fabrizio, and the moment they'd switched on the light, both Dooley and myself found ourselves simply sitting there and staring—like a pair of deer in the headlights!

Big mistake.

"Aaaaargh!" Maisie screamed.

"Cats!" Fabrizio hollered, as if we were the ultimate horror.

And then they were crawling out of bed and grabbing for anything they could find to throw at us!

Now the sight of humans in a state of undress is terrible enough in the best of times, but when they have murder on their minds, as these two clearly had, it's much, much worse!

Humans, you see, are not covered in fur, like cats are. While our physique is nicely concealed, providing an excellent esthetic, they have all their dangly stuff on full display.

Talk about a horror movie!

So Dooley and I screamed probably as loud or even louder than this twosome, and then made a beeline for the open window where we planned to make our speedy escape.

Unfortunately the Blandines had other plans. While Mr. Blandine cut off our avenue of escape, Mrs. Blandine had found a broom with which she seemed intent on hitting us where it hurt. Moments later, she had us cornered, and things looked very bleak indeed! It wasn't helped by the sight of all of her wobbly bits jiggling and joggling like crazy!

"Max! Over here!" suddenly a voice rang out. I looked past Maisie Blandine, still brandishing her broom, and saw... Brutus!

And then our friend let rip the most terrifying growl I've ever heard in my entire life!

It sounded like a mixture of a wolf and a lion, and had a profound effect on Maisie.

She whirled around and hollered, "Fabrizio! There's another one over there!"

"It's a cat infestation!" Fabrizio cried, grabbing his hair in clear distress.

To the left of him, suddenly Harriet materialized, and she let out a caterwaul louder even than Brutus's war cry! Between the two of them, they produced the kind of noise that could inspire Stephen King to write a dozen novels and adapt them into movies, too.

With Maisie and Fabrizio on their toes, Dooley and I managed to reach the window, and as we watched, Harriet and Brutus beat a strategic retreat, the humans in the room too stunned now to mount an effective defense against this attack of the feline brigade.

Moments later we had all hopped it to the soft grassy lawn below, and ran as fast as our paws could carry us. We only stopped to catch our breath three backyards down the road, and I couldn't help but give both Harriet and Brutus a look of intense gratitude.

"You saved our lives," I said, panting heavily. "Without you guys we would have been caught!"

"Yeah, they had us cornered," said Dooley.

"Why didn't you wait for us?" Harriet asked, slightly peeved.

"What do you mean?" I said. "I thought you didn't want to come."

"Of course we wanted to come. But first I wanted a bite to eat," said Brutus.

"And I needed to tinkle," said Harriet. "Never leave home without a tinkle."

I slapped my brow. "I thought you were afraid to head out so soon after that suicide mission with the duck people."

Harriet gave me a smile. "Max, haven't you learned anything? Brutus and I will always have your back, no matter what."

"Yeah, we like to bitch and moan, but at the end of the day we're there for you," Brutus chimed in.

I have to say their words brought tears to my eyes. Though it could have been the close escape we'd just had that made me uncharacteristically emotional all of a sudden.

"Dust in my eye," I murmured.

"Oh, Maxie baby," said Brutus, and actually gave me a hug!

"So what have we learned?" asked Harriet.

"That Maisie and Fabrizio are having an affair," I said.

"United in their grief, they must have found each other," said Dooley.

Somehow I had my doubts about that. But it did confirm a suspicion I had.

Which meant we hadn't risked life and limb for nothing. At least I hoped we hadn't!

CHAPTER 33

Chase wasted no time. The sun wasn't even up yet when an impressive contingent of police officers surrounded the house where Maisie Blandine lived. Fabrizio's car was still parked in the driveway, so the bird hadn't yet flown the nest.

When the door opened and Maisie appeared, looking a little bleary-eyed and with a nightgown wrapped around herself, she blinked and said, "What's going on?"

Chase held up a piece of paper and said, "This is a warrant to search the premises, Mrs. Blandine. Are you alone in the house?"

"Um..."

Behind her, Fabrizio now also appeared, looking equally knackered. You can't spend half the night doing the horizontal mambo and the rest chasing a small contingent of feline intruders and not expect to feel the strain.

"What's all this?" asked Fabrizio.

"Have you moved in with your sister-in-law, sir?" asked Chase.

"Of course not. What kind of a question is that?" Fabrizio blustered.

"Fabrizio and I stayed up late, planning my husband's funeral," said Maisie, having recovered from the surprise of finding Chase on her doorstep. "And since it was late by the time we finished, he decided to stay over."

"And before you jump to any conclusions, I slept in the spare bedroom," said Fabrizio.

"Of course you did," said Chase, and stepped past the unlikely couple. About a dozen more cops followed in his footsteps, and while two officers kept a close eye on Maisie and Fabrizio, the rest all fanned out and started searching the house top to bottom.

"Now this is what I had in mind," I told Dooley, "but before you can search a place, you need to have a good reason. Or in police parlance, probable cause."

"And does Chase have a good reason now?" asked my friend.

"Let's wait and see," I said, and stretched out on the front lawn next to the boxwood while the search was in progress. There wasn't anything we could do, after all, and another close encounter with Maisie and Fabrizio was the last thing either of us wanted.

Odelia had also driven up, and now joined the search. She'd brought Harriet and Brutus, and the four of us settled in for a long wait.

As the sun pulled on its big-girl pants and painted the world in a roseate hue, neighbors up and down the street came out of their houses to take in all the police activity, and before long, spectators had gathered in front of the house, talking amongst themselves and speculating freely about what was going on here.

In other words: free entertainment for young and old.

Suddenly a voice upstairs called out, "Chief! Over here!"

We all perked up at this, and so did the crowd, three deep now, all craning their necks to see what the upshot was of all this shouting. Judging from their expressions they fully expected some bloodied corpse to be carried out of the house at any moment.

Odelia now appeared in the door and beckoned us over.

And so we entered the house, a small procession of cats, and joined Chase and Odelia in the living room, along with Maisie and Fabrizio, who looked very antsy indeed.

"I demand an explanation!" said Fabrizio.

"You can't do this to me," said Maisie. "I just lost my husband. I deserve some respect!"

But instead of respect, Chase held up two mobile phones, both neatly sealed inside an evidence bag. At the sight of the phones, Maisie's face went a little pale, and so did Fabrizio's.

"I told you to get rid of those!" Fabrizio snapped.

"I was gonna! But with all these cops around, I couldn't!" Maisie returned.

"We've checked the phones," said Chase, "and found the message you sent to your husband on the evening of his murder. A message for him to meet you at the Poltorak farm."

"So? It's not a crime to meet your husband," said Maisie, but she looked shifty now.

"I think we'll find your husband's fingerprints on the other phone, which is the one you gave him, isn't it?"

But Maisie pressed her lips together, and crossed her arms in front of her chest.

"Here's what we think happened," said Odelia. "You and Fabrizio were having an affair, and you had been thinking about divorcing Eric for a while now. So when the offer came for Eric to replace Cotton Karat while he was in therapy for his sex addiction, you saw an opportunity to get rid of your husband, and get some money out of this deal, too."

"You knew that the Karats would do anything to avoid

the whiff of scandal," Chase said as he placed the phones on the table in front of the duo, "and so you hatched a brilliant scheme. You bought two phones so you and Eric could stay in touch when he assumed the role of Cotton, and told him to meet you that night out by the Poltorak duck farm. And since Eric always did what you told him to do, he dutifully showed up for the meeting."

"We're not exactly sure which one of you actually killed him," said Odelia. "But we think it was probably a joint effort. Eric had told you about the threats made against Cotton's person by the Duck Liberation Front people, and so you made it look as if they were behind the murder. You killed your husband, cut out his liver and delivered it to the Karat Group headquarters with a note, claiming responsibility for the DLF."

"A nice touch, I have to say," said Chase. "In fact the whole setup was brilliantly conceived and carried out."

"Which is when we come to the second part of your plan. You blamed the Karat Group for Eric's death, accusing them of not keeping him safe, and threatened to take them to court, all the while knowing full well they'd settle out of court before that happened."

"I talked to Tobias Pushman just now," said Chase, "and he confirmed that he reached a settlement with you yesterday, for a total sum of three million dollars. Not a bad haul for a woman who set up and murdered her own husband, wouldn't you say, Maisie?"

Maisie's face spelled storm now, and she was freely glowering at Chase and Odelia.

"Don't say a word, Maisie," Fabrizio warned. "They've got nothing on us. Nothing."

"We've got these phones," said Chase. "They prove that it was actually you who lured your husband to his death. They place you at the scene of the crime and not, as you claimed, here at the house. And then of course there's this." And like a trained conjurer, he produced from behind his back another plastic evidence bag, this one containing a long, serrated knife with a red handle. And if I wasn't mistaken, there was blood on the blade.

"Oh, God," said Fabrizio, as he buried his head in his hands.

"I told you, I was waiting for these coppers to get off our backs!" Maisie burst out.

"Stupid, stupid, stupid," Fabrizio moaned.

Suddenly Maisie's eye shifted to me and she frowned. "Hey," she said, pointing in my direction. "That's the same orange fatty that was in here last night!"

At this, I drew myself up to my full height and said, rather haughtily, I'm afraid, "For your information, my name isn't Fatty. It's Max, and I'm not orange—I'm blorange!"

CHAPTER 34

"Eric Blandine was one of those people who wouldn't say boo to a goose," I said.

"Why would anyone want to say boo to a goose, Max?" asked Dooley.

"It's just an expression, Dooley. Nobody actually says boo to a goose."

"I wouldn't mind saying boo to a goose," Brutus grunted. "Teach them some manners."

Brutus had once been chased by a goose, and evidently the experience still rankled.

We were in Tex and Marge's backyard, where a party was in full swing. Ever since Gran had given up trying to force the vegetarian lifestyle on the rest of the family, it was almost as if the sun had come out and I'd rarely seen the Pooles as happy as now.

It's like wearing a pair of tight shoes: the moment you take them off, it's liberating.

"So Eric Blandine was a man who wouldn't say boo to a goose," Harriet reminded me.

"Yes, thank you," I said with a grateful smile in my friend's direction. "So when he suddenly decided to ignore the instructions Tobias Pushman had given him about keeping a low profile and showed up at Merle Poltorak's farm in the shank of the evening, there had to be a good reason. And that got me thinking about the man's psychology. Why would a man as meek as Eric Blandine ignore a direct order from a man who was basically his boss's boss? A man who ordered him not to show his face anywhere?"

"Because his wife had told him to," said Harriet with a nod of satisfaction. "See, pookie? A good man always does what his girl tells him to."

"And gets murdered in the process," Brutus muttered, earning himself a scowl from Harriet.

"But how had Maisie reached her husband? There were no messages on his phone, no emails, no phone calls. So it stood to reason that before sending him on his mission, she must have given him a secret phone so they could stay in touch throughout."

"But how did you know she hadn't dumped those phones?" asked Brutus.

"I didn't, obviously, but I was hoping she hadn't. And as it turned out, she hadn't gotten rid of the murder weapon either."

"That wasn't very smart of her," said Harriet. "She should have dumped the weapon on the night of the murder, and the phones."

"She didn't want to risk the knife or the phones being found," I said. "So she decided to keep them for now, until she could figure out a way to get rid of them for good. She never thought anyone would suspect either her or Fabrizio, so she felt pretty safe."

"How long do you think their affair had been going on?" asked Harriet.

"A couple of months at least, maybe even years. But as long as there was no financial incentive, they weren't too bothered to make things official. That all changed when Eric was asked to replace Cotton. Suddenly there was a good reason to get rid of the man."

"Three million reasons, in fact," said Brutus, nodding.

"Who do you think killed Eric?" asked Harriet. "Maisie or Fabrizio?"

"They were in it together," I said. "As it turns out, Fabrizio used to work for a butcher in a distant past. An experience that came in handy now."

Dooley shivered. "What a terrible duo," he said. "Imagine cutting out a man's liver."

"Yeah, it needed to be done that way to throw the police off their scent," I said. "Though I very much doubt they took any enjoyment in the act of murder. But in the end the combination of love and money as a motive was simply too powerful to resist."

The sweet smell of grilled meat wafted in our direction, and my stomach juices immediately responded. The humans seemed eager to dig in, too, for they all sat casting anxious glances in Tex's direction from time to time, satisfying themselves with some appetizers for now. Finally Uncle Alec couldn't take it anymore, and joined his brother-in-law at the grill, vouchsafing a steady flow of meaty treats later on.

"So what's going to happen to the Karat Group?" asked Charlene, popping an olive into her mouth. "Is Cotton going to be in charge from now on or his brother Jared?"

"They seem to have decided on a joint chairmanship," said Odelia. "With the necessary checks and balances in place so that Cotton doesn't mess things up again."

"And Ebony Pilay?" asked Marge. "Is she still Cotton's girlfriend?"

"Ebony is out of the picture. Though a little birdie told me that Ebony and Zak Lemanowicz are dating again."

"Oh, how romantic," said Scarlett. "The supermodel and the pig farmer."

"Duck farmer, Scarlett," said Gran. "Not pigs."

"Ducks, pigs, same difference," said Scarlett.

"I think you did a great job," said Charlene, addressing Odelia. "Again, I might add."

"It's all Max," said Odelia. "He's the one who figured it out."

"Imagine that," Uncle Alec grunted. "A cat who solves crime. If you told this to anyone they wouldn't believe it."

"I believe it," said Charlene, throwing a smile in my direction. "He's a smart cookie, that cat of yours."

"Cats, plural," I corrected the Mayor. "I couldn't have done it without my friends. Or Odelia and Chase, of course."

"Yeah, it's a team effort," said Gran. "We all chipped in this time. Scarlett and I went undercover in Lita Fiol's outfit, Odelia and Chase did the legwork, and Max sat back and let that big brain of his compute all the evidence and come up with the perfect solution."

"What I find fascinating," said Marge, "is that Lita Fiol and Tobias Pushman are an item. They seem like such an unlikely couple."

"Opposites attract, Marge," said Charlene. "Haven't you learned that by now?"

She was right, of course. Let's examine the evidence: Marge and Tex. Odelia and Chase. Charlene and Uncle Alec. Harriet and Brutus.

Even among friends the same truth applies: Gran and Scarlett. Me and Dooley. Or even all four of us. Brutus and I couldn't be more different. Or Dooley and Harriet. And still we're the bestest of friends. Sometimes we fall out, but in the end, friendship prevails.

And as the pleasant banter slowly lulled me to sleep, suddenly a loud cry had us all look up. It came from Odelia, who'd jumped up from her chair and was staring at something on her plate. And as I looked closer, I saw that it was something… hairy!

"Dad!" she cried. "What do you think you're doing!"

Tex immediately came hurrying over, and picked up the offending food item between thumb and forefinger. It was a bug. A very big, hairy bug.

"I didn't put that there," he said. "I draw the line at bugs, honey."

"They are very nutritious, though," Gran knew. "Plenty of protein."

"I don't care about protein!" Odelia cried.

"Well, you should. Pregnant women need lots of protein."

"Did you put that bug on my plate?" Odelia demanded hotly.

"Of course not!" said Gran. "Though, like I said, they're very healthy. And yummy."

"Vesta, tell me you didn't," said Charlene.

"Oh, for crying out loud. If I had put that bug on your plate I would have fried it first."

"Fried it!" Marge cried.

"Did you know that fried bugs are considered a superfood? They even turn them into hamburgers now. Though in Japan they like to eat their bugs alive. Yummy for your tummy!"

And as the recriminations shot back and forth, suddenly something dawned on me. I slowly turned to Dooley, and when I saw his apologetic smile, the penny dropped.

He gave me a penitent shrug. "What can I say, Max?" he said quietly. "It's my USP."

Oh, boy. It was going to be a long nine months.

THE END

Thanks for reading! If you want to know when a new Nic Saint book comes out, sign up for Nic's mailing list: nicsaint.com/news

EXCERPT FROM PURRFECT DATE (MAX 47)

Chapter One

It was book club night at Tex and Marge's place—though Tex was conveniently elsewhere, since he wasn't a member—and the house was cozily busy. Marge, as Hampton Cove's librarian, did the honors as usual, in the sense that she picked the book, sent out the invitations and supplied the necessary refreshments for the participants, and I must say she did a great job.

Her daughter Odelia was there, of course, and so was our mayor, Charlene Butterwick. The other members were unknown quantities as far as I was concerned, but I still viewed them with the kind benevolence of a cat who knows that treats will be forthcoming and cuddles given—all in moderation, of course.

The book Marge had chosen was *Tears in the Mud* by Jacqueline B. Wilding, a torrid tome of love and loss, and clearly the participants had all enjoyed the book tremendously, as evidenced by the glowing comments they awarded it.

EXCERPT FROM PURRFECT DATE (MAX 47)

All in all, as far as I could tell, book club was mostly an excuse to get together and gossip, while enjoying free cake, tea and cookies, but then who am I? Just a lowly feline observer that nobody pays too much attention to—apart from said treats and cuddles.

Book club membership currently stood at eight. Which meant that apart from Marge, Odelia and Charlene, five other ladies had decided to show up. They were, reading from left to right: Emma Kulhanek, who was a sort of mousy-looking housewife, Lynnette Say, also a housewife, but more of the glamorous 'The Real Housewives of New York City' type, Adra Elfman, an elderly lady who was also a regular at the library, Carlotta Brook, who ran our local archery club and was allegedly a crack shot with bow and arrow, and of course the rising star in our local business community: the one and only Valina Fawn.

You may have heard of Valina. You may even have signed up for the dating site she runs, also called Valina Fawn, and one of the better-known and successful dating sites out there right now. Forget about Tinder or OkCupid or any of those highfaluting apps. Valina Fawn is the site both the loveless and the hopeful all turn to when looking for love.

"Is it true that the President himself found the First Lady on your site, Valina?" asked Adra Elfman now. The old lady sat nibbling a chocolate chip cookie and looking at Valina with delight. It wasn't too much to say that one of the main reasons Marge's book club meetings were so popular lately was exactly because of Valina's star quality. Though of course the lady knew discretion was key, and kept her trade secrets very much to herself.

"That would be telling, Adra," said Valina, who was a strikingly handsome woman in her early forties. Her straight blond hair was coiffed to perfection, and as usual she was dressed in one of her trademark power suits. "And as you know, a lady never tells."

"So it's true," Adra murmured, her eyes shining brightly.

"I very much doubt whether the President found his wife on a dating site," said Lynnette. "I'm sure he's got better things to do than to trawl those awful sites—no offense, Valina."

"None taken," said Valina graciously. She knew better than most that the notion of finding love on the internet still carried a certain stigma, and worked hard to erase it.

"It's exactly because the President has so many things on his mind that he doesn't have time to go out and find himself a partner," said Emma Kulhanek. "The man is so busy all the time I can easily imagine how he would turn to a dating site to find love again." She smiled a little smile as she demurely crossed her fingers in her lap. "In fact I think you're providing a wonderful service, Valina. To bring people together is an act of compassion."

Lynnette glanced over to Emma. For some reason the two ladies had never got on. Perhaps because Lynnette saw herself reflected in Emma, though in a more banal way. "You would say that, Emma," she said. "You're exactly the kind of person Valina caters to."

Emma frowned. "And what kind of person is that, may I ask?"

"Well, the hopeless romantic, of course."

"There's nothing wrong with being romantic," now Charlene piped up. "In fact it's romance that provides a glimmer of hope for humanity."

"Which brings us right back to our book," said Marge, managing a nice segue.

"Didn't you and Valina go to school together, Emma?" asked Carlotta Brook. The archery club's chairwoman was tall and boyishly coiffed, and had at one time been a professional archer, even going so far as to earn herself an Olympic medal in her chosen discipline. She still had the sinewy athleticism that had served her so well, as well as the no-nonsense attitude.

"Yes, we did," said Valina, who'd been checking her phone. "Seems like such a long time ago now, doesn't it, Em?"

Emma smiled. "It certainly does. Though having kids of my own, it all seems to come back to me. Especially since they're going to the same school we went to. Though it's all quite different now, of course. Especially since I'm teaching at the very school I was a student at."

"Hard to credit that you're both the same age," said Lynnette, glancing from Emma to Valina. "You seem so… different."

Emma's smile wavered. "If you're trying to tell me I look old, you can come right out and say it, Lynnette. No need to beat about the bush."

"Ladies, ladies," said Odelia, holding up her hands like a referee. "We're all friends here. All united in our appreciation of fine literature?"

There were murmurs of agreement, though judging from the looks Emma was shooting in Lynnette's direction, it was clear that the latter's insensitive remarks would be addressed at a later date.

"Is it true that George Clooney found his Amal through your site?" asked Adra, who'd dipped in and had secured herself another chocolate chip cookie. The old lady clearly was more interested in any gossip Valina was willing to dispense than in fine literature.

"That would be telling, now wouldn't it?" said Valina finely.

"George doesn't need a dating site," said Carlotta. "That man had to fend off the women throwing themselves at his feet back in the day. With all the ladies vying for his attention he could have started a dating site on his own, with him the only male."

"Is there anyone here who actually found love through a dating site?" asked Lynnette. "And it doesn't have to be Valina's site, though of course hers is the Rolls Royce of sites." She gave the businesswoman an ingratiating look. "I'll go first, shall I?" she immediately added. "I responded to some of those dating ads in the paper once—your paper, actually, Odelia—but unfortunately found them slim pickings. The men I ended up going out with were all horribly uncouth, I must say." She slightly tilted her chin. "Dross of mankind."

"So how did you find Franco?" asked Charlene, referring to Lynnette's husband.

"Quite the old-fashioned way, actually," said Lynnette. "We bumped into each other at a fundraiser for orphaned kids. He had just bid on a marvelous Willem de Kooning, and I had bid on an amazing Jackson Pollock, and when we went backstage to make the necessary arrangements, we got to talking. His views on life and art perfectly matched with mine, and so when he asked if I wanted to see his art collection, of course I said yes."

"You're sure he was referring to his art collection and not something else?" said Emma.

Lynnette shot a look that could kill in her fellow book club member's direction and shrugged. "You don't have to tell us how you met your hubby, Em. I'm sure it's a story so saccharine it'll make our teeth hurt."

"It wasn't through a dating site, if that's what you mean," said Emma, bridling a little. "But it was a romantic tale, that's true. When our school needed a new online learning platform, Norwell was the man in charge of design and construction. So we got to work together very closely indeed. And during one of those late-night meetings I suddenly realized that I was looking forward to seeing him

EXCERPT FROM PURRFECT DATE (MAX 47)

much more than I should. And as he later admitted, he felt exactly the same way. Three months later we were married."

"And how about you, Odelia?" asked Valina. "How did you and Chase meet?"

"Through work, I guess," said Odelia. "He was this cocky cop who'd joined our local police force and hated me meddling in police affairs. So we ended up crossing swords quite a lot, even as we tackled some of the most baffling murder cases. But once I saw past his cockiness, and he got down from his high horse... Well, we just hit it off."

"Oh, how romantic!" Adra cried. "And so much more interesting than discussing a boring book, wouldn't you say?"

"Odd that they would get together for book club and think talking about books is boring," said Dooley, who was lying on the couch next to me.

"I'm sure they'll get around to discussing the book eventually," I said, though clearly Marge wasn't holding out hope, as evidenced by the fact that she'd already put her copy of the book down and was sitting back, resigned to listen to stories about first meets.

"I guess when you and Tex first met dating sites weren't around yet, were they?" asked Lynnette, addressing their fearless book club leader.

"Not sites as such," said Marge, "though just like you I did respond to an ad in the paper. Though when I say responded, it would probably be closer to the truth to say that my mom responded and then guilted me into going. You see, I'd just broken up with my boyfriend, and was feeling a little down in the dumps, and Ma thought I needed cheering up."

"Mom!" said Odelia. "You never told me you met dad through a personal ad."

"Well, I did," said Marge. "He was a medical student back then, and one of his fellow students had actually sent in that ad, so when he showed up for our date he was less than

EXCERPT FROM PURRFECT DATE (MAX 47)

excited, feeling he had to go through with it, or be accused of being disloyal. And since I felt exactly the same, it wasn't a propitious start. But much to our surprise, we hit it off immediately, and have been together ever since." She smiled at the recollection. "Though I'm not sure my mother still doesn't regret setting us up for that date."

"Are you kidding?" said Charlene. "Any mother would kill to see her daughter go off and marry a doctor."

"I know, but my previous boyfriend was the son of a local millionaire businessman, so in my mother's view a mere doctor was a step down in my fortunes. Though I never saw it that way. Also, my former boyfriend is in prison now for kidnapping his own wife, so it's safe to say my mother's views on him have since gone through a major modification."

They all laughed at this, but then Valina's phone chimed and she got up. "I'm sorry, but I have to take this," she murmured, and hurried off into the kitchen. We heard her talking rather heatedly into her phone, but then as more people shared the details of their love life with the others, we forgot all about Valina and her urgent call. Until, that is, she came hurrying back into the living room to grab her coat. "I have to go, Marge," she said, shooting a look of apology in the latter's direction. "Something came up at the office."

And without further ado, she shot out of the room like a flash.

"What kind of an emergency can there be with a dating app?" asked Carlotta laughingly.

"A bad match?" joked Charlene.

"Or maybe the site has gone haywire," said Lynnette. "And people are all being forced to swipe left when they want to swipe right. Or is it the other way around? I'm not well-versed in the latest minutiae of dating, and glad of it, too, if you want to know." She performed an exaggerated eye roll. "I'm just happy I found my perfect match before the days of

EXCERPT FROM PURRFECT DATE (MAX 47)

internet dating became the hype *du jour*. It all seems so complicated now!"

"Doesn't it just," said Adra. She held up her hand and flicked her wedding ring. "Been married fifty years this autumn. Hard to believe it's been that long."

"So how did you and Gene meet, Adra?" asked Carlotta.

The old lady's eyes flickered. "In a book club just like this one, only a slightly saucier one I must admit. It was one of those underground book clubs that focused on the racy kind of book. Most of the members were women, of course, but there was one brave soul who'd ventured into the unknown, though he was under the impression it was a Jane Austen book club. Until he discovered the kind of books we were reading. He gamely went along, though, and soon was the center of attention, of course. The only man in a club full of women. Later on he told me that he liked me from the first. And I must say I fancied him, too. Especially since he had such a nice voice when he read out those long erotic passages from *Lady Chatterley's Lover*!"

More laughter filled the room, and I slowly drifted off to sleep.

Marge's book club members may love to share stories of first love, but frankly the only story I'm interested in is the story of my perfect couch. Talk about love at first sight!

Chapter Two

By the time I opened my eyes again, all book club members had mercifully dispersed, and Marge and Odelia were gathering cups and saucers and carrying them into the kitchen. A strange sound reached my ears, and when I looked over, I saw that Harriet was sitting nearby, hovering over a tablet computer and deftly swiping it with her paw pads. The sound that had roused me from my nice nap was Harriet

EXCERPT FROM PURRFECT DATE (MAX 47)

quietly but with rising intensity saying, "No, no, no, no, no! How is this possible!"

I gave her a lazy look. "What's wrong?"

"Oh, it's this new dating app," the pretty white Persian said. "I can't make heads nor tails of the thing."

Dooley had to laugh at this. "Heads nor tails," he said. "Funny." When Harriet shot him a withering glance, he weekly added, "Tails. Because you have a tail?"

"Oh, Dooley," Harriet grumbled, then frowned some more at her tablet.

Brutus, who'd wandered into the kitchen, looking for a bite to eat, now returned. "Stay out of the kitchen," he said. "It never ceases to amaze me how people who love books can make such a mess. Marge and Odelia have been doing the dishes for what feels like hours."

"It's because Marge likes to show off by taking out her finest China," I explained. "And since she can't put them in the dishwasher they all have to be washed by hand. And with special detergent that doesn't cause any damage. And all hand-dried very carefully and replaced in the cupboard, lest they might chip."

Brutus had hopped up onto the couch next to his mate and now frowned at the tablet. "What is this?" he asked.

"Nothing special, sweetie," said Harriet. "Just some app I'm trying out."

"Is that… Pettr?" asked Brutus, sounding aghast.

"What's Pettr?" I asked.

"It's like Tinder for pets," Brutus explained. "You swipe right when you have a match." He now took a closer look at the app his lady love was surfing on. "It *is* Pettr. Why are you on Pettr?" he demanded.

"I was just curious, sugar babe," said Harriet. "Shanille told me about it, and so I wanted to take a look. Just to know what all the fuss was about."

EXCERPT FROM PURRFECT DATE (MAX 47)

"Shanille is on Pettr?" asked Brutus.

"Yeah, she is."

"What is a dating app, Max?" asked Dooley.

"It's an app where people looking for a partner find each other," I said.

"How does it work, exactly?"

"Well, you create a profile on the site or the app, with a picture that was taken twenty years ago, then you write something about yourself, usually painting yourself in a more favorable light, and then you hope that someone who comes across your profile likes it enough to swipe right and give you a try. And if you like the person who swiped right, you can also swipe right and you arrange to meet."

"So you don't look like you, and write stuff that isn't really you, and the other person does the same?" said Dooley, catching on quickly.

"That's about the gist of it," I agreed.

"But won't the other person notice that you lied?"

"Of course they will, but you hope that social pressure will prevent them from walking out on you in the middle of a busy restaurant, and that through the sheer magnetism of your personality you'll be able to make them forget you're twenty years older and thirty pounds heavier, and that you're not as fascinating as you made out to be in your profile."

"Sounds like a recipe for disaster," was my friend's estimation.

"And yet sometimes it seems to works," I said.

"And sometimes it doesn't," said Harriet, and gave us all a sad look. "I accidentally swiped right when I should have swiped left. So now what?"

"Now you're going on a date," I said cheerfully.

"What?!" Brutus cried. "No way!"

"I'm sorry, sunshine," said Harriet. "I got confused."

"Between left and right?!" he asked, incredulous.

EXCERPT FROM PURRFECT DATE (MAX 47)

"I mix up left and right all the time," said Dooley.

"So who did you match with?" asked Brutus. Then, as he took a closer look, he gasped in shock. "No way!"

"Who is it?" I asked, my curiosity aroused in spite of myself. But all I got were blank looks from both Harriet and Brutus.

"It'll be fine," said Brutus. "You simply stand him up, that's all."

"It's not going to be good for my rating," Harriet said.

"Who cares about your rating!" He eyed her suspiciously. "Unless you want to keep on dating?"

"Of course not, snuggle bear! Like I said, I was just taking a look."

"That's fine, then," said Brutus, though he didn't seem entirely convinced. Then again, if I found my girlfriend creating a profile on a dating site, I wouldn't be convinced of her innocence in the matter either.

"Is Pettr the same site our humans were talking about earlier?" asked Dooley.

"No, that was the human version. It's called Valina Fawn," I said. "Named after the site's founder and president Valina Fawn."

"It's so interesting to have a real celebrity in our midst," said Dooley now, as he placed his head on his front paws. "So did she really set George Clooney up with Amal?"

Oh, God. What was the world coming to when even Dooley was starting to spread celebrity gossip?

Just then, there was a loud crashing sound coming from the kitchen, followed by irate voices. Moments later, Tex walked into the living room. His face was red and he had a hunted look on his face. "Who puts their best China on a table in front of the kitchen door?" he muttered, then sank down on the nearest couch and turned on the television. A dating show was in full progress, so he decidedly flipped the

EXCERPT FROM PURRFECT DATE (MAX 47)

channel until he'd landed on the Discovery Channel, which was showing a documentary about the migratory pattern of the native geese. Tex relaxed and moments later was in a deep sleep, and so were we.

Chapter Three

On Saturday morning at the Brookwell Archery Club, three familiar figures were having a whale of a time. They were Tex Poole, his son-in-law Chase Kingsley, and Tex's brother-in-law Alec Lip. All three men were holding bow and arrow, but so far they hadn't exactly been successful in hitting their targets, which had been set up a little ways away —at any rate too far away for them to hit them. Then again, they probably would have had a hard time hitting anything unless it was three feet away.

Archery is a demanding sport, after all, and only through diligent practice can one hope to get any good at it. And since the only reason Tex, Chase and Alec were members of the club was because the price of the lukewarm beer they served in the clubhouse was the best price in town, they didn't stand a chance of ever going to the Olympic Games.

Carlotta Brook herself was there, of course, and so was Carlotta's husband Dennis, who was in charge of the club's financial side: collecting membership fees and such. And it was with exactly this important task in mind that he now set foot for Alec Lip and discreetly led the police chief away from the others.

"I see you haven't paid your fees yet this month, Alec," Dennis said, lowering his voice when discussing this oh-so-delicate matter with the errant member in question. "If you're having trouble, we could maybe set up a payment plan? Easy weekly installments?"

"That won't be necessary," Alec grunted, looking a little

annoyed. "Just a minor oversight, that's all." And when the other man stared at him, he added, with a touch of incredulity. "Surely you don't want me to pay you now, Dennis?"

"If you could. You can call me nitpicky, but I like everything to be just so."

"Oh, all right," said Alec, and took out his wallet to pay the man. He quickly glanced over, but both Tex and Chase had discreetly turned their heads the other way. No one likes to intervene in a close relative's financial affairs. That way only trouble and strife lie.

Once Tex had settled up, he rejoined the others, and as they stood sipping from their lukewarm beers, and idly gazing at the target somewhere in the distance, they talked about this and that, happy for this chance to shoot the breeze and strengthen those all-important bonds of friendship.

"So book club last night, huh?" said Chase. "How was it? Odelia wouldn't tell me."

"Plenty of gossip, from what I understand," said Tex. "Emma Kulhanek and Lynnette Say locked horns again, and Adra Elfman wanted to know how the others had all met their significant other. Marge was annoyed, I can tell you that much. She spends a lot of time preparing for these weekly meetings, and when all is said and done, nobody reads the book, nobody is interested in discussing the book, and the only thing she takes away from the meeting is the minutiae of everyone's love life, which isn't exactly the point."

"I'll bet it's more interesting than the book itself," said Alec with a grin. "Why did Emma and Lynnette lock horns?"

"Lynnette seems to think Emma is too dowdy for book club. She wants to raise book club's profile, and Emma isn't a good fit. With Charlene she has the mayor, Marge is a doctor's wife, Odelia is a prominent reporter, Carlotta is an

EXCERPT FROM PURRFECT DATE (MAX 47)

Olympian and plays an important role in the local community as a Rotary Club member, and of course runs the archery club, and then there's Valina Fawn, who's a major celebrity in her own right."

"So where does Adra Elfman fit in?" asked Chase. "She's hardly a celebrity."

"Adra's husband Gene was the long-time chairman of the Chamber of Commerce," said Alec. "And he's still very well connected, even though he's now retired, of course."

"But isn't Emma's husband something big with Valina Fawn's site?" asked Chase.

"Norwell is a developer," said Tex. "So in Lynnette's eyes he's a computer geek."

"He's more than just a developer," said Alec. "Norwell is Valina's business partner."

"And Emma is a teacher, which isn't the kind of person Lynnette wants to be seen associating with," said Tex, shrugging his shoulders.

"In other words, Lynnette Say is a big, fat snob," said Chase.

"A snob with a lot of money, and since Marge is always on the lookout for people interested in donating to her library…"

Just then, Chase's phone chimed, and he took it out. He frowned at the display. "Did you guys see this? Looks like Valina Fawn has been hacked."

"Valina Fawn or her site?" asked Tex.

"The site." Chase's frown deepened. "Uh-oh. The hackers have put a list with the names of all of Valina Fawn's customers online."

And as they glanced around, suddenly phones of other members started beeping frantically. And as men took out their phones, faces blanched, muttered curses were uttered, strangled cries emitted, and before long a minor stampede

EXCERPT FROM PURRFECT DATE (MAX 47)

was in motion, with people hurrying off to the parking lot and making a hasty departure.

When the dust had finally settled, the only ones left were Tex, Alec and Chase... and of course Carlotta and Dennis Brook. Though the latter looked very much ill at ease as he came face to face with his wife.

Carlotta stared at her husband with ill-concealed rage displayed on her sinewy face. Then she hauled off and hit him squarely in the stomach and walked off on a huff.

Dennis, who'd doubled up and staggered back, now stared at the departing image of his wife, his hand massaging his injured midsection, clearly stunned by this development.

Alec shook his head. "I just hope this won't lead to any problems," he said.

"Pretty sure it will," said Chase, and drained the last of his beer. He frowned when his own phone chimed, and took it out. "Family meeting—now!" he read from the display. He looked up to find both his father-in-law and uncle-in-law gazing at their own phones.

All three men shared a look.

The trouble had begun.

ABOUT NIC

Nic has a background in political science and before being struck by the writing bug worked odd jobs around the world (including but not limited to massage therapist in Mexico, gardener in Italy, restaurant manager in India, and Berlitz teacher in Belgium).

When he's not writing he enjoys curling up with a good (comic) book, watching British crime dramas, French comedies or Nancy Meyers movies, sampling pastry (apple cake!), pasta and chocolate (preferably the dark variety), twisting himself into a pretzel doing morning yoga, going for a run, and spoiling his big red tomcat Tommy.

He lives with his wife (and aforementioned cat) in a small village smack dab in the middle of absolutely nowhere and is probably writing his next 'Mysteries of Max' book right now.

www.nicsaint.com

ALSO BY NIC SAINT

The Mysteries of Max
Purrfect Murder
Purrfectly Deadly
Purrfect Revenge
Purrfect Heat
Purrfect Crime
Purrfect Rivalry
Purrfect Peril
Purrfect Secret
Purrfect Alibi
Purrfect Obsession
Purrfect Betrayal
Purrfectly Clueless
Purrfectly Royal
Purrfect Cut
Purrfect Trap
Purrfectly Hidden
Purrfect Kill
Purrfect Boy Toy
Purrfectly Dogged
Purrfectly Dead
Purrfect Saint
Purrfect Advice
Purrfect Passion

A Purrfect Gnomeful

Purrfect Cover

Purrfect Patsy

Purrfect Son

Purrfect Fool

Purrfect Fitness

Purrfect Setup

Purrfect Sidekick

Purrfect Deceit

Purrfect Ruse

Purrfect Swing

Purrfect Cruise

Purrfect Harmony

Purrfect Sparkle

Purrfect Cure

Purrfect Cheat

Purrfect Catch

Purrfect Design

Purrfect Life

Purrfect Thief

Purrfect Crust

Purrfect Bachelor

Purrfect Double

Purrfect Date

The Mysteries of Max Box Sets

Box Set 1 (Books 1-3)

Box Set 2 (Books 4-6)

Box Set 3 (Books 7-9)

Box Set 4 (Books 10-12)
Box Set 5 (Books 13-15)
Box Set 6 (Books 16-18)
Box Set 7 (Books 19-21)
Box Set 8 (Books 22-24)
Box Set 9 (Books 25-27)
Box Set 10 (Books 28-30)
Box Set 11 (Books 31-33)
Box Set 12 (Books 34-36)
Box Set 13 (Books 37-39)
Box Set 14 (Books 40-42)
Box Set 15 (Books 43-45)

The Mysteries of Max Big Box Sets

Big Box Set 1 (Books 1-10)
Big Box Set 2 (Books 11-20)

The Mysteries of Max Shorts

Purrfect Santa (3 shorts in one)
Purrfectly Flealess
Purrfect Wedding

Nora Steel

Murder Retreat

The Kellys

Murder Motel
Death in Suburbia

Emily Stone

Murder at the Art Class

Washington & Jefferson

First Shot

Alice Whitehouse

Spooky Times

Spooky Trills

Spooky End

Spooky Spells

Ghosts of London

Between a Ghost and a Spooky Place

Public Ghost Number One

Ghost Save the Queen

Box Set 1 (Books 1-3)

A Tale of Two Harrys

Ghost of Girlband Past

Ghostlier Things

Charleneland

Deadly Ride

Final Ride

Neighborhood Witch Committee

Witchy Start

Witchy Worries

Witchy Wishes

Saffron Diffley

Crime and Retribution

Vice and Verdict

Felonies and Penalties (Saffron Diffley Short 1)

The B-Team

Once Upon a Spy

Tate-à-Tate

Enemy of the Tates

Ghosts vs. Spies

The Ghost Who Came in from the Cold

Witchy Fingers

Witchy Trouble

Witchy Hexations

Witchy Possessions

Witchy Riches

Box Set 1 (Books 1-4)

The Mysteries of Bell & Whitehouse

One Spoonful of Trouble

Two Scoops of Murder

Three Shots of Disaster

Box Set 1 (Books 1-3)

A Twist of Wraith

A Touch of Ghost

A Clash of Spooks

Box Set 2 (Books 4-6)

The Stuffing of Nightmares

A Breath of Dead Air

An Act of Hodd

Box Set 3 (Books 7-9)

A Game of Dons

Standalone Novels

When in Bruges

The Whiskered Spy

ThrillFix

Homejacking

The Eighth Billionaire

The Wrong Woman

Made in the USA
Las Vegas, NV
29 August 2023